DEAD
FIREFLY

Also by Victoria Houston

Dead Spider

Dead Loudmouth

Dead Rapunzel

Dead Lil' Hustler

Dead Insider

Dead Tease

Dead Deceiver

Dead Renegade

Dead Hot Shot

Dead Madonna

Dead Boogie

Dead Jitterbug

Dead Hot Mama

Dead Frenzy

Dead Water

Dead Creek

Dead Angler

DEAD FIREFLY

A Loon Lake Mystery

VICTORIA HOUSTON

G

GALLERY BOOKS

New York   London   Toronto   Sydney   New Delhi

G

Gallery Books
An Imprint of Simon & Schuster, Inc.
1230 Avenue of the Americas
New York, NY 10020

First Gallery Books trade paperback edition June 2018

GALLERY BOOKS and colophon are registered trademarks of Simon & Schuster, Inc.

For information about special discounts for bulk purchases, please contact Simon & Schuster Special Sales at 1-866-506-1949 or business@simonandschuster.com.

The Simon & Schuster Speakers Bureau can bring authors to your live event. For more information or to book an event, contact the Simon & Schuster Speakers Bureau at 1-866-248-3049 or visit our website at www.simonspeakers.com.

Interior design by Davina Mock-Maniscalco

Manufactured in the United States of America

10   9   8   7   6   5   4   3   2   1

Library of Congress Cataloging-in-Publication Data

Names: Houston, Victoria, 1945- author.
Title: Dead firefly / Victoria Houston.
Description: First Gallery Books trade paperback edition. | New York : Gallery Books, 2018. | Series: Loon Lake mystery ; 19
Identifiers: LCCN 2017060944 (print) | LCCN 2018004925 (ebook) | ISBN 9781440598890 (ebook) | ISBN 9781440598876 (softcover : acid-free paper)
Subjects: LCSH: Ferris, Lewellyn (Fictitious character)—Fiction. | Osbourne, Doc (Fictitious character)—Fiction. | Policewomen—Wisconsin—Fiction. | City and town life—Fiction. | BISAC: FICTION / Mystery & Detective / Women Sleuths. | FICTION / Crime. | FICTION / Mystery & Detective / General. | GSAFD: Mystery fiction.
Classification: LCC PS3608.O88 (ebook) | LCC PS3608.O88 D429 2018 (print) | DDC 813/.6—dc23
LC record available at https://lccn.loc.gov/2017060944

ISBN 978-1-4405-9887-6
ISBN 978-1-4405-9889-0 (ebook)

For Mike

I think we are well-advised to keep on nodding terms with the people we used to be, whether we find them attractive company or not.

Joan Didion
(on the importance of keeping a notebook)

CHAPTER ONE

Doc Osborne relished the final swallow of his fourth cup of coffee before pushing his chair back from the kitchen table. Time to get down to work. He had insisted Lew hurry off to her morning meeting and let him take care of the dishes.

Nothing better than a slow start to a sunny summer day, he thought, especially after sharing a good night's sleep with the woman who had changed his life. He leaned over to stack the breakfast dishes before standing up coffee cups in one hand and plates in the other with knives and forks on top. He turned back toward the kitchen sink.

Whoa. Startled, Osborne dropped the cups, which shattered across the tile floor. A man, his face framed in the window over the sink, stood staring at Osborne. It took a moment for Osborne to realize he knew the face.

"Chuck?" he asked, his voice hesitant as he wondered how long the man had been there: silent, watching.

Setting the breakfast plates down, Osborne hurried through the mudroom to hold open the back door. Chuck Pelletier was standing among the waist-high forsythia bushes Osborne's late wife had painstakingly planted along the back of their lake house.

"Chuck? Are you okay? How long have you been standing there? Why didn't you knock? For heaven's sake, don't just stand there—come in. Please."

Chuck Pelletier was the lead accountant for Northern Forest Resorts (NFR), a real estate development project owned by a hedge fund out of New York City. The project was an ambitious effort to turn ten thousand acres of woods and water into a luxury bird hunting and fly-fishing preserve modeled after New Zealand's Huka Lodge. Millions of dollars had been poured into purchasing the land, and now the hard work of stabilizing riverbanks and restoring spring creeks along with building lodges, cabins, and service buildings—not to mention a first-class wine cellar—was under way.

But Osborne had gotten to know Chuck through a very different venue, one having nothing to do with water, woods, and certainly not wine. Once a week the two met behind the door with the coffeepot on the glazed glass window: they were members of a private club dedicated to keeping the names of its members secret: Alcoholics Anonymous.

"Thank you," said Chuck, his voice low and serious as he walked past Osborne into the kitchen, where he sat down at the table, which still held juice glasses. Osborne took a moment to kick shards of the broken coffee cups to one side before taking the chair across the table from his visitor, who was sitting with his back straight, hands resting on his knees as he stared down at the tabletop. Osborne sensed Chuck was bracing himself to speak.

"Hey, bud," said Osborne, urging in an understanding tone. "What is it? Are you drinking?"

"No."

"Do you feel you need a drink?"

"No."

Osborne waited, watching. Chuck was casually dressed in crisp khaki fly-fishing pants and a long-sleeved light gray-and-blue-checked shirt. He might have been on his way to a Trout Unlimited meeting.

"Well, what . . . why—"

Chuck raised his head, his eyes meeting Osborne's as he said in a matter-of-fact voice: "My wife and Gordon Maxwell tried to kill me this morning. I was walking up my driveway after checking for the mail when the two of them in his SUV tried to run me over."

CHAPTER TWO

Osborne's turn to stare: Had he heard right?

Thirty years of dealing with patients in his dental office on matters ranging from the private ("I'm afraid I see signs of an STD in your mouth . . .") to the irritating ("Your child refuses to behave while in my dental chair. I insist you find another dentist . . .") had not prepared him for anything like Chuck's allegation. Not even the heartrending confessions heard in AA.

"Chuck, why tell *me*? You should be going to the police."

"With my record?" said Chuck with a snort. "They wouldn't believe me. Doc, I've got two DUIs on my record. They'll think I'm drunk—or hallucinating."

"But—" Osborne started to interrupt, eager to remind his friend that he had had no issues with alcohol in the almost two years since his marriage.

"No," said Chuck, shaking his head as he raised both hands to quiet Osborne. "Please. Listen to me. I've heard you say you've been deputized to help out the Loon Lake Police when dental forensics are needed and that you know the chief of police pretty well. . . ."

"True."

"So I thought, since you know me, too, and better than most people"—he spoke with a grimace that acknowledged their shared experience seeking solace in the bottle—"that you have to be the best person for me to tell. The cops will listen to *you*, right?" The hope in Chuck's eyes was naked.

"Maybe they will," said Osborne, desperate to be helpful but still bewildered by what his friend had said. "Why don't we drive into town together and meet with Chief Ferris and, you're right, she is aware that you and I have a lot in common. . . ."

———

That was true: both men were in their early sixties, both had lost wives to whom they had been married for decades, both had daughters, and like Osborne, Chuck was a tall, lanky man who still had all his hair. But those details aside, shortly after they'd met in the AA room six months earlier, he and Osborne had been quick to recognize that they shared something else: a love of the outdoors and fishing.

For Chuck it was fly-fishing, a sport he had pursued since his teens growing up on the Beaverkill in the Catskills. Once he heard that, Osborne had invited his new friend to his home to share grilled bratwurst and fly-fishing stories. For Osborne a highlight of the evening had been showing off the new Winston fly rod to which he had just treated himself and a dozen trout flies tied especially for him by someone whose name he was hesitant to mention.

But it was when Osborne was describing his frustration learning how to double haul fly line that Chuck learned that Doc's fly fishing instructor, Lewellyn Ferris ("Chuck, you wouldn't believe it. I thought I had signed up to take casting lessons from a guy named 'Lou,'" Osborne had said with a grin), was also Loon Lake's chief of police.

Left unsaid that evening, however, was the fact that Osborne's instructor (also the source of his precious trout flies) had become a regular at his breakfast table—and vice versa. But then he assumed Chuck had been around enough to figure out the breakfast scenario on his own. Apparently he had.

Over the coming months, as the two men got to know each other, Osborne learned they shared quite a bit more than a love of fishing and a determination to survive their addiction.

Chuck had lost his first wife to cancer just three years earlier and, like Osborne after Mary Lee's bronchial infection turned deadly, had fallen into an alcoholic swoon immediately afterward. But he was recovering—and changing his life.

Not only had he accepted a generous financial offer from the hedge fund developing the Partridge Lodge Fishing and Hunting Preserve to become the chief financial officer on the project—but he also had been able to purchase on the nearby lake a lovely home into which he had moved with a new bride. A fractured life restarted.

Osborne knew he had two adult daughters, who sounded like strong-minded young women. The daughters had collaborated to force their father into an intervention that saved his life—again, an experience he had in common with Osborne.

But new beginnings are not guaranteed to work perfectly: Chuck's grief from the loss of his late wife remained so raw that it could surface at unexpected moments, which happened the evening Osborne introduced him to the Prairie River.

That night, as the two men waded under a star-studded sky, Chuck paused to gaze overhead. After a long moment, he said, "Lois would have loved a night like this, Doc. She was an expert fly fisherman—better than me, in fact.

"You know," he'd said with a grudging grin, "women are naturals in the trout stream. You and me—we try to muscle that trout fly while they just let it go as if releasing a butterfly. Yep, Lois and I met in college and the minute I heard she loved to fly-fish, I was a goner. Just watching her cast . . . Doc, that woman moved with such grace. . . . "

Tears had shimmered unexpectedly, and Chuck, knee-deep in riffles, had choked out, "My God, you wouldn't believe how I miss that woman. She"—his voice had faltered—"she laughed at all my stupid jokes, Doc. Even when she'd heard them seventeen times before. God, I miss that laugh."

"But you've found someone," said Osborne, anxious to help him through the moment, "and moving on is healthy, Chuck, even if it is . . . different."

"*Different?*" Chuck had given a wry smile. "Patti is different all right. Yes, she's younger and energetic, but she doesn't *get it*, not like Lois and I did." Raising his right arm to cast, he said, "I made a mistake getting married again. I'll live with it, but my advice to you when you're tempted to remarry, *if* you're tempted: *Don't compromise*. It's not worth it."

Observing Chuck from where he sat across from him at the kitchen table, Osborne recalled it was Chuck who had characterized his second wife, Patti, as "energetic." Maybe she was too energetic? But trying to run over your husband? That didn't make sense.

"I do think you're wrong about the police not listening to you, Chuck," he said, convinced there was more to Chuck's story. "Think about it: here in Loon Lake you are highly respected. People are impressed with the Partridge Lodge, and you play a major role in that—"

"I'm just the goddamn bookkeeper," said Chuck angrily. "Gordon Maxwell is running the show. He's the guy spreading a hundred million bucks around. Not me. Who the hell is going to listen to a bookkeeper whose wife has decided to screw the big dog?"

"Okay, I get your point," said Osborne. "But at the risk of sounding like an idiot, can you give me some idea why your wife and Maxwell would go to such an extreme?"

Chuck shook his head as he said, "I have no idea. I mean if the woman wants a divorce, all she has to do is ask me, you know?" The despair in Chuck's eyes worried Osborne. There was no mistaking he believed two people had tried to kill him.

"Look, I'm calling Chief Ferris," he said, getting to his feet. "You have to tell her what—"

Before Osborne could say more, Chuck's cell phone rang. He pulled it from his shirt pocket and, looking down, jumped to his feet. "Oh God, I have to go, Doc. I forgot I have a nine o'clock conference call with New York. But I'll be back right after the call. I just . . . don't have the time right now. Don't worry," said Chuck with a quick clutch of Osborne's shoulder as he hurried by. "I'll be safe."

"But, Chuck, I really—"

The man was gone. Through the kitchen window Osborne

saw him dash for his car. Sitting back down at the kitchen table, Osborne pondered what had just happened. He was baffled: something didn't make sense. He got up to reach for the broom and sweep up the broken pottery littering the kitchen floor but stopped midway to the broom closet. He had to alert Lew: Chuck was not hallucinating.

CHAPTER THREE

Too anxious to wait for Chuck to return, Osborne decided to call Lew right away. He punched in the number for her personal cell phone and waited. Within seconds his call went to voice mail. Darn, he thought, remembering as he waited that Lew had planned to attend a multicounty meeting with law enforcement and Department of Natural Resources (DNR) personnel.

He left the message: "Please call. Got an emergency."

The meeting, which had been called at the last minute, was the reason Lew had rushed into her office earlier than usual. As she was leaving she had mentioned that it was scheduled to last several hours, which meant she and Osborne would have to skip their usual midmorning coffee break. The subject was a bizarre series of thefts occurring across northern Wisconsin. The stolen goods? Birch trees.

Lew was particularly interested, since her department had received twenty-three calls in less than a week from Loon Lake property owners reporting that someone had cut down trees on their land without permission. At first, assuming the usual illegal logging for firewood, Marlaine on Dispatch had neglected to ask for more details. But calls back to the owners clarified that the damage had been done to birch trees exclusively, and the problem appeared to be escalating.

Osborne knew Lew would not want to miss that meeting—but what was more important: a dead tree or a dead person? He decided it was worth risking her irritation if only for a moment to be sure he and Chuck would be next on her list.

Before he left for town, Osborne made one more call. He wanted Chuck to know where he was headed, why, and when he would be back. Chuck's secretary answered the call: "I'll let Mr. Pelletier know to call you the minute he's off that conference call, Dr. Osborne, but I'm pretty sure it'll be another forty-five minutes at least. These calls with the New York office run long."

That did it. Osborne decided not to wait. He'd drive to the county courthouse, where Lew was in her meeting, and persuade her to take a break or, at least, whisper in her ear. Once she heard what had happened to Chuck, Osborne was sure she would want to see him ASAP. If Osborne moved quickly, the three of them could meet back at his house within an hour.

Stepping into the backyard, he called Mike. The black Lab bounded from the far corner of the backyard where he had been conducting surveillance on a rambunctious chipmunk teasing him from the other side of the fence. Hooking the dog onto the yard leash, Osborne gave him a quick pat and said, "Mike, you're in charge. Watch the house for me, will you?"

With soulful eyes, the dog acknowledged his responsibility then circled twice before settling down on a cushion of pine needles.

Climbing into his car, Osborne was relieved to see he had

plenty of gas to make it to town and back. This was one morning he did not want to waste time at the gas station.

No sooner had he turned onto the county road than he spotted a turtle in the middle of his lane inching its way toward the shoulder on a mission to lay eggs. With too much oncoming traffic to swing out and around the creature, he had no choice but to brake and wait.

And breathe in the soft summer air. In spite of Osborne's concern for Chuck—and the turtle—he couldn't overlook the beauty of the day. As he waited he studied the balsams lining the road. Refreshed by spring rains and with boughs no longer straining under the burden of wet snow, the trees stood like robust teenagers: shoulders back, spires reaching for the sky.

Three long minutes passed before the turtle was safe on the shoulder and Osborne could take his foot off the brake. He hadn't gone five hundred yards before a doe leaped from a clump of bushes on his right to dart in front of the car. Osborne hit the brakes and waited, certain a fawn was likely to follow. After a moment and confident that wasn't the case, he was about to press down on the gas pedal when a gang of turkeys waddled onto the road from the left. Traffic in both directions came to a halt.

Only in the northwoods, thought Osborne with a shake of his head as he wondered if it would be possible to reach the courthouse before the end of the damn month. He checked his watch. He had half an hour before Chuck might make it back to his house. Good thing he lived seven minutes from town.

———————

"The murder weapon is a chain saw," said the DNR conservation officer who was running the meeting. "The thieves go in wherever they see birches—state, county, federal, private land—doesn't matter to them, if they find a grove where they can cut a lot of trees in a short time."

"Have you been able to catch any of these people?" The question came from the back of the room, and Osborne, who had just crept in through a side entrance, recognized the voice: it was Lew asking the question.

"Only seven so far, and we know there are a lot more out there doing this because of all the missing trees," said the officer. "Used to be small-timers supporting drug habits, but this is on a much larger scale.

"That's why we're here today. We think there may be an organized effort going on and you people may be able to help us put a stop to this. If you see what looks like an unusual logging site, please check it out to be sure it wasn't a couple hundred birches that were stolen."

"All this for home decor? You mean those cute little logs that hold candles on the dining room table?" asked another audience member.

"The size of the market for these trees has surprised us," said the DNR officer, "used to be people stole spruce branches at Christmas, but this is on a much larger scale. Stores buy them, interior designers, wholesalers for the hobby market. People like them in their outdoor containers as well as indoors in homes and offices. The birches are a hot item right now—a huge and growing business that has caught us by surprise."

As she listened to the discussion and watched slides of sites where dozens of trees had been chopped down, Lew had a sudden thought. She raised her hand. "I think I've had birches stolen off my land," she said. "It's an area in the far left corner of my property where I thought I had wind damage but these photos are making me think. . . ."

"Okay," said the officer, "here's what to look for. The thieves who know what they're doing go after young birch that are ten to fifteen years old, about two to four inches in diameter, and ten to eighteen feet tall. They take those and leave the stumps.

"Chief Ferris, the wind does not leave sawn-off stumps. Is the area you're talking about pretty secluded?"

"Now that you mention it, yes," said Lew, "which is why I haven't walked back in there."

"Can someone get a four-wheeler or a truck in there without you seeing?"

Lew nodded. "Easily."

"Then get out there and take a good look at your land. You may not be happy with what you find—or don't find." With a grim smile, the officer turned to take another question.

"How long does it take for the birches to grow back?" asked a woman who was sitting close to where Osborne was standing at the back of the room. He had hesitated to approach Lew during this part of the discussion. He knew she wanted to hear every word; he did, too.

"That's part of the problem. Assuming a birch sapling isn't squeezed out by fast-growing aspen and other aggressive shrubs, it will take a good ten to fifteen years for that tree to grow back. And the shame, aside from the obvious damage to property, is that losing young birch hurts the deer that browse on young forests along with songbirds like pine siskins and chickadees, for whom the young twigs, buds, and seeds are a critical food source.

"Folks, we're talking about an illegal harvest of potentially monumental proportions and one that will have a long-term negative impact on our northwoods' environment. We need your help badly."

———

Lew was sitting straight up, eyes and ears glued to the discussion, when she felt a tap on her shoulder. "Lew?" Osborne whispered from where he was standing near an empty chair behind her. He beckoned with one finger for her to follow him out of the room. The expression in his eyes alarmed her and she got to her feet even as she kept her eyes on the slides being shown on the large screen at the front of the room.

"What is it, Doc?" she asked once they were outside the meeting room. He spoke fast.

"Okay," said Lew, "I'll be out to your place as soon as I can alert the office where I'll be."

"Good," said Osborne, "see you there." He hurried toward the door to the parking lot.

Reluctant to leave the presentation on the birch trees but understanding Osborne's concern, Lew stepped back into the conference room and picked up a printout with the DNR officer's name and contact information. She had heard enough to know she needed to get home to her farm and check out the back forty as soon as possible.

CHAPTER FOUR

Striding into Osborne's kitchen with a harried look on her face, Lew yanked a kitchen chair out from under the table and plunked herself down. Her obvious frustration, which was unlike her, worried Osborne. This was a woman he had known to tackle the most exhausting, if not dangerous, situations with a stoicism he had to admire. Right now, if something was bothering her, he was sure it had to be his fault.

"Sorry about asking you to drive all the way out here, Lew, but I know this is serious. Chuck isn't the type of person to overreact."

"Doc, I know you well enough to trust your judgment," said Lew, leaning forward, elbows on the table, fingers intertwined. "Believe me, I am very interested in what he has to say. And I want to check out his property—the driveway in particular.

"I hate to say this," she said, sitting back with an apologetic shake of her head, "but your friend's wife could indeed be having an affair with this Maxwell person, and the two of them could indeed have been rushing to get her home before her husband suspected anything. But trying to run him over? That could have happened by accident. It wouldn't be the first time. . . ."

"I hope you're right," said Osborne, knowing as he spoke that he doubted Lew's scenario. But he didn't argue. They would find out soon enough. Instead, he set two cold cups of coffee in the microwave, hit the START button, and sat down to join her at the kitchen table.

Lew shifted in her chair to sit sideways with her left elbow resting on the tabletop. She crossed and uncrossed her legs three times. "You're nervous," said Osborne. "Is it this meeting with Chuck? I've never seen you so jumpy."

"No, it isn't your friend." A morose look swept across Lew's face. "But once I have a better handle on what's happening with him, I need to run out to my place. I think I'm one of the people who've had birch trees cut down and stolen. In fact, the more I think about it, the surer I am. But," she said with a wave of her hand, "that damage is done. Getting there sooner rather than later won't make a difference, so I need to settle down. Is that coffee ready?"

"Not sure *that's* the answer," said Osborne with an understanding pat on her shoulder as he handed her a cup of hot coffee.

The New York hedge fund had arranged for Gordon Maxwell and Chuck Pelletier to lease a small office building abutting the Partridge Lodge development properties. The building, less than ten years old, had decent Internet and phone systems—a benefit for which Chuck gave thanks every time he walked in. Good cell service, not to mention a reliable Internet connection, was hardly the norm in the northwoods, where you can drive a quarter mile and lose even your ability to call 911.

Hurrying into the conference room just minutes before
New York was scheduled to call, Chuck was relieved to see
that Gordon wasn't there. No surprise, really. Gordon liked to
brag to investors and contractors that "*I'm* the big-picture guy.
My buddy, Chuck here, handles the small stuff, the day-to-day
bullshit. You know how it goes. All those details can get so
complicated they get in the way of critical decision making."

Too complicated? Really? Chuck kept his mouth shut but
each time he heard Gordon say that, he wondered if the real
reason was that the man couldn't read—much less understand—
financial statements.

Not having Gordon on the conference call that morning
was also fine with Chuck because it meant he wouldn't have
to listen to the excuses he suspected would be made regarding the episode earlier that morning: "Hell, Chuck, you got
that blind curve on your driveway. I didn't see you till the
last minute. . . ."

And why was Patti in his car? Chuck found it easy to
imagine that excuse: "On my way to the office, she waved me
down in front of the fitness center—her battery was dead. Just
being a Good Samaritan, y'know."

If he'd been forced to listen to that baloney, Chuck would
have nodded in understanding, hiding the fact that he knew
the truth. In one fleeting instant he had seen the look of grim
determination on Gordon Maxwell's face as he drove at him:
the man had known exactly what he was doing.

Waiting for the call from the hedge fund executives,
Chuck struggled to get his mind on the reports in front of
him. Experience had taught him the health of a project was in
the details—"the small stuff." A long career as "the numbers

guy" on the building of seven hotels, two airports, twelve churches, and numerous commercial buildings had taught him what to look at and why.

Unlike Gordon, he prided himself on being an expert on reading financial reports. More than once his expertise in discovering buried cost overruns and kickback schemes had saved a project from going bankrupt.

As it was, one bridge and connecting roadway under construction for the Partridge Lodge development had caught his attention: the cost of supplies and contractor fees were mounting at such a rate that he had half-humorously called Gordon on it saying, "These costs are so high, makes me wonder—are we building a bridge to nowhere?" Gordon, who had recommended that particular contractor, had promised to look into it.

Once the conference call started, Chuck was able to focus as he and the two financial managers who were based in the hedge fund's home office reviewed the status of construction under way on the main lodge, a network of new roads being designed to look like ancient logging lanes, an assortment of service buildings, two stream-rebuilding projects, and three bridges—along with the contractor fees, invoices for supplies, bids needing to be posted, and, finally, the selection of construction materials made by various contractors.

Here was where Chuck kept a close eye in order to flag kickbacks. It wasn't unusual for a contractor to bill for quality goods but, instead, purchase substandard materials and pocket the difference. Chuck knew he wasn't popular among some of the local contractors when he questioned such purchases, but it wasn't his job to be liked.

One of the finance guys on the call mentioned the high

cost of the bridge that Chuck had questioned. "Yes, I'm wondering about those costs, too," said Chuck. "I've asked Gordon to look into it, as he signed that contract. Should hear something in the next day or two."

Once the call ended, and even though Chuck knew he needed to get back to Osborne's ASAP, there was one last item he wanted to check on while Gordon was out of the office.

He pulled up Gordon Maxwell's résumé: the one posted on the Partridge Lodge website, the one designed to impress potential investors and, eventually, guests willing to pay twenty-five-hundred dollars a night to sleep, eat, hunt, or fish at the Partridge Lodge. At Chuck's request, his secretary had been able to find an e-mail address for one of Gordon's partners on a past project—a condo complex with an attached shopping mall in Naples, Florida, which (according to Gordon) was a huge financial success.

After identifying himself and his role in the Partridge Lodge project, Chuck e-mailed a series of questions to the former partner. Hiding his questions in wording that was matter-of-fact and businesslike, he hoped to learn if Gordon Maxwell had been the "big-picture guy" on that project, too. Deliberately disengaged from the day-to-day details, the nitty-gritty of finances and planning? How had they used his talent for planning such a massive undertaking?

Of course the questions he really wanted to ask but didn't dare were just two: Did Gordon Maxwell's résumé exaggerate his role in the Florida project? Had he lied?

To cover his reason for e-mailing the partner, Chuck explained that he was leading a review of the Partridge Lodge project's organizational chart and wanted to be sure the management team maximized Gordon's role.

After sending that e-mail and as he was heading for his car in the garage, Chuck made a mental note to call his lawyer immediately after the meeting with Doc Osborne and Chief Ferris. For the first time since his marriage to Patti, he had the urge to be sure his daughters were protected financially should something happen to him. Molly and Jessica didn't need to find that Patti, his wife of less than two years, had inherited the bulk of his assets.

———————

It wasn't only what had happened that morning that had him thinking about Patti and their marriage. In the last few months, he had been learning more about her in little ways. For example, her hysterics when he criticized her for spending twenty thousand dollars on a stove they didn't need. "Honestly, Chuck," she had wept, "you can't expect me to be a good cook on an *electric* stove!"

While he agreed she was an excellent cook—early in their relationship her apple pie had been way too seductive—he knew gas stoves didn't have to cost that much. Nor did they really need to spend a hundred thousand dollars on furniture for the new house. After all, he and Lois had owned beautiful antiques, furniture he loved and that was now buried in the basement.

But maybe it was discovering that while he loved to read books on the outdoors, on history and politics, even crime fiction—Patti devoured romance novels. Only romance novels. When she wasn't watching *Real Housewives* on TV.

Small grievances, he knew, but they were adding up to feelings of resentment if not downright dislike. Until this morning he had been trying not to admit the obvious: he had made a big mistake.

———————

Chuck hurried into the office building's attached garage, where he was privileged to have one of three parking spaces for senior executives. Parking in the garage kept his car out of the hot sun, which he appreciated, since he liked to keep a fly rod, his fly-fishing vest, and a couple boxes of trout flies in the SUV—always hoping to escape the workday for an hour or two of fly-fishing.

Reaching for the door on the driver's side, he was surprised to find it unlocked. He must have been so preoccupied that morning he forgot to lock it, something he usually did automatically. As he slid into the driver's seat he checked his watch. Good, he would be back at Osborne's within twenty minutes.

After latching his seat belt, he was reaching overhead for the button that opened the electric garage door when he felt something hard and cold press against the back of his neck.

A nasal whisper he didn't recognize gave him directions.

CHAPTER FIVE

When forty-five minutes had passed and they were still sitting at the kitchen table with no sign of Chuck, Osborne was ready to give up. "Damn it, Lew," he said. "I am so sorry about this. I was sure Chuck would be here by now."

He picked up their empty coffee cups and set them in the sink. "I'll try his office and cell phone once more and if I don't reach him this time, you should go."

When Chuck didn't answer his cell phone, Osborne tried the office number. "No, Dr. Osborne, Mr. Pelletier hasn't been back," said the secretary after Osborne apologized for calling her a third time. "Like I said before, he left the office over an hour ago."

Setting down his cell phone, Osborne glanced over at Lew before saying, "Something doesn't feel right. He was so shaken this morning. I'm sure he would call me if he's changed his mind."

"Doc, so much emotion is involved in situations like this," said Lew. "Could be he wants to sit down and talk with his wife before he raises legal issues that could complicate both their lives. You don't accuse someone of attempted murder without being sure. . . ."

"I know, I know," said Osborne. "Look, you go check on your property and I'll drive over to Chuck's place. I'd like to be sure he's okay."

"No. That is not wise, Dr. Osborne," said Lew, addressing Osborne in the tone she used for bad actors. "This is a couple who may be having a hard time and you need to stay out of it. If there's anything those of us in law enforcement approach with extreme care, it's domestic *disturbances*." Osborne got the message.

"Promise me you'll wait here until you hear from your friend. Okay? Agreed?" Osborne nodded and Lew got to her feet. He could tell she was anxious to get out to her place.

"Agreed, Chief Ferris," said Osborne with a rueful smile. "I'll call you the minute I hear from him."

Osborne watched Lew's cruiser back out of his driveway. He decided to wait thirty more minutes before trying Chuck's cell for the fourth time. But half an hour later, there was still no answer.

That's it, thought Osborne, I'll just drive by the house and see if his car is there. If the car is there, I'll relax and mind my own business.

But there was no "driving by" the Pelletier home, as it was set back so far from the main road that neither house nor garage could be seen. A stand of pines hid the property from anyone driving along the main road.

Osborne decided to drive in a short ways, enough to get a quick look. That was a mistake. As he came around a blind curve, he found himself in front of the house, where Patti was watering pots of petunias lining the sidewalk. She glanced up with a smile and waved.

Too late, thought Osborne. He better come up with a good story. Also, he wondered if Chuck's car might be in the garage, the entrance to which faced away from the front of the house.

"Hello, Doc," called Patti as he got out of his car. "What brings you out here? Chuck isn't home. You can find him at the office."

"I tried there but he was out," said Osborne. "I was hoping he was here so we could finish planning a fishing trip up to the Middle Ontonagon River this Saturday." It was a lie but it worked.

———

Osborne did not find Chuck's wife attractive. He had met her only twice before and each time he couldn't help but notice her eyes, which appeared bulbous under streaks of black lining the lids top and bottom. Her eyebrows were penciled on with the same heavy black line. That plus a long nose over lips smeared an unnatural shade of scarlet prompted an unkind thought: the woman reminded him of a monkey.

Before retiring from his practice, when he had female patients who wore that much makeup, he had the urge—also unkind—to caution them about getting in a boat. Mrs. So-and-so, he would think to himself, if you were to go overboard wearing all those cosmetics, you might sink.

———

Osborne turned back to his car, ready to leave, now that he knew Chuck wasn't home. But Patti had other plans. After setting down her watering can, she sidled over to him, gazing up with a coy smile, eyes lowered seductively. Osborne found the coyness irritating. All he had wanted to know was if her husband was home.

"Chuck should be home for lunch soon. Come on out to the patio—let me get you an iced tea," she said, batting the awful eyes.

"Thanks, Patti, but I'll check with him later," said Osborne, climbing into his car. He put the car into reverse, gave a quick wave, and headed back down the long, curving driveway toward the main road.

Now he was more worried. Where *was* his friend?

The house sat on five acres and he knew from a previous visit with Chuck that there was a back road that led to a small, abandoned barn. They had walked the road one day and Chuck had shown him the barn. It was where he stored two float tubes and an impressive collection of fly-fishing gear. He had even outfitted a small room for tying trout flies: "Quiet out here, Doc. No TV." It was obvious he used the barn as a retreat.

As he drove over a berm, Osborne spied the barn with Chuck's SUV parked in front. With a sigh of relief—and not a little irritation—Osborne pulled alongside Chuck's car.

CHAPTER SIX

After alerting Dispatch that she was taking an early lunch break, Lew drove out to her farm. Continuing west past her driveway, she slowed, checking for signs of vehicles having been driven across the gully that ran along the county road in front of her property.

When she had reached her neighbor's driveway with no sign of tire tracks, she turned around to head back, driving slow, eyes scanning the weedy shoulder. This time she thought she could see a matted-down patch of wildflowers where wheels of some kind had traveled along the gully before turning up toward a large sumac.

Lew pulled over and got out of her cruiser. She pushed past the sumac and looked down. Something had flattened the vegetation fronting a wall of aspens, something heavy moving in search of an access to the birches growing behind the dense border of aspen. A pickup? An ATV? She couldn't be sure of the vehicle but one thing she was sure of: someone had driven onto her property without permission.

When she had purchased the farm and its eighty acres ten years earlier, she had been pleased to find that the aspens were not only great cover for grouse but they also screened acres of birches and other hardwoods—leafy havens for birds. Or they *had* screened the trees.

Pushing past the aspen, she found herself looking at a scene of devastation similar to what she had seen on the DNR's slides of sawn and stolen birches earlier that morning: foot-high stumps and torn strips of birch bark littered a vast open space. Young saplings, not birches, which had been pushed aside, tipped crazily in the now open areas. No wonder that when she had peered across the field and into the woods from a distance, she had thought she was looking at wind damage.

Lew ran back to the cruiser, sat down, and pulled out the DNR officer's business card from the small leather case in which she kept IDs and other critical information. She called his cell number, got his voice mail, and left a message with her name, her address, and the approximate location of the stolen trees. After leaving the message, she sat silent, thinking.

She made another call: she wanted those tire tracks photographed before a rainstorm washed them out. Likely they were already too faint to be identified but she would like to at least try to determine if it had been a pickup or an ATV that had trespassed. And there was one person likely to know.

"Ray," she said, reaching voice mail once again, "I need you to photograph tire tracks on my property. Right along the county road and just west of my driveway. Whoever it was trespassed on my land and cut down dozens of birch trees. The sooner you can do this before it rains, the better. I'm hoping that eagle eye of yours can tell if the tracks belong to a truck or an ATV or whatever.

"Please, Ray, take two hours off from your fishing and I'll

make it worth it." She tried to laugh at the end of her message but she sounded strangled instead.

Her cell phone rang two minutes after she finished leaving the message. "Ray? That was fast. Are you out on the lake?"

"No, Chief, I'm on my way back from . . ."—Lew held her breath waiting—"the Lake . . . Tomahawk . . . Meat Market."

"Ah," she said in a fruitless effort to rush him along.

"Yep . . . owed the man . . . a basket of . . . blue . . . gills for the great, great bratwurst he sold me last weekend."

Lew listened patiently. Everyone in Loon Lake listened to Ray patiently. At least everyone who knew him, and that was almost everyone. A happy Ray had the most annoying habit of elongating his commentaries so that two-syllable words could end up with four, and one brief sentence could seem like a never-ending paragraph. But as everyone said, "That's Ray—but he has a good heart."

"Say," Ray said, speaking a little faster, "I listened to your message and I have my camera in the truck. Thought I'd stop on my way by your place in about fifteen minutes . . . and see what I can see."

"Look for the big sumac just before my fire number," said Lew, "that's where I spotted tracks and if you follow them up and past the aspens, you'll see why I'm worried."

"Ten four," said Ray, "gotcha covered."

Ray Pradt might own a misdemeanor file an inch thick in her Loon Lake Police Department desk drawer—thanks to an affection for cannabis—but Lew had learned to depend on the young fishing guide who knew his way through woods and along lakes and rivers as keenly as the Native Americans who had hunted and fished through the same territory.

More than once she had deputized him to help with searches and to photograph crime scenes. Perennially short of cash because of the vicissitudes of guiding when big muskies proved too elusive, Ray augmented his income two ways: one, he took photos of outdoor vistas for a local insurance agent's annual calendar; and, two, he dug graves at St. Mary's Cemetery. While he had learned the hard way he couldn't count on fish showing up when needed, he was pretty certain seasons would change and people would die. At least he hoped.

Minutes after talking to Ray, Lew pulled up in front of her little farmhouse. Climbing out of the cruiser, she realized she was trembling. The theft of the birches may have taken place a good quarter mile from her home but she felt as shaken as if someone had crept into her bedroom through the dark shadows of night, crept in, and touched her body: she felt violated.

"For God's sake get a grip, Ferris," she muttered out loud. "It's only trees." She pushed open the front door of her home and walked in. Everything inside looked just as she'd left it the day before. And then it didn't.

The landline base was blinking with a message. Lew stared at it, trying to remember who on earth had this number. The ancient portable phone was for the landline, which she kept only because it could be relied on during a power outage. Unlike her cell phones of which she had two—one personal and one for the police department—it was not dependent on fiber-optic cables. But the landline was so old not even Osborne had that number.

Must be some goofy sales call from India, she thought as she hit the ON button.

"Lewellyn," said a shaky, thin voice on the line, "dear? Please help me. I've been robbed." Aside from leaving a phone number, those few words were all that were spoken.

Lew set the phone down, thinking. Was that really Lorraine? Maybe some sort of telephone scam? She replayed the message. It was Lorraine, all right. Lew knew the voice though she hadn't heard it in years: Lorraine Gropengeiser, her former mother-in-law. The woman had to be in her eighties and they hadn't spoken since Lew walked out on her son. How odd that she would call her now.

Lorraine lived in a modest two-bedroom house on a narrow channel that connected two large lakes at the outskirts of town. The channel—a playground for otters, ducks, great blue herons, and turtles—had enchanted Lew's son and daughter when she left them with their grandmother while she worked as a secretary at the paper mill.

The house with its perennial need for a new roof and other repairs may have struck some people as a "teardown," but the land on which it sat was close to priceless: level, dry, and within minutes of the best muskie and walleye fishing in the county. It also bordered the new Partridge Lodge development, which added even more to its value.

Lew remembered Lorraine, who'd been widowed for years, as a quiet but self-sufficient woman—carrying in her own firewood for the woodstove that heated her little place, driving her Honda Civic to Eagle River for bingo at the senior center twice a week, and crocheting baby hats for the Episco-pal Church's women's group. She may have been uneducated but she was organized and careful—her house spotless, her garden a blooming delight.

———————

Though they had had their differences during Lew's marriage, Lew had an abiding affection for the older woman. She did not hesitate to return the call.

"Lorraine, I got your message. *What on earth?* Did some-one break into your house? Are you okay?"

"I am okay. I mean, physically okay," said the slow, familiar voice. "But I'm not really. My girlfriend, Gloria, told me to call you. Maybe you can help—I don't know what to do. It's one of those things, you know?"

No, I don't know, thought Lew, resisting the urge to hurry her along. "I'll do my best. Tell me what's wrong."

"They stole my house, my flowers, my wonderful sand beach—it's all gone."

"Back up, Lorraine. I don't understand. How could anyone steal your house?"

"They told me they were going to dam Sand Lake, so my place would be underwater. They said the county board would condemn my property and I wouldn't be able to sell it no way. So I had to take what they offered. . . ."

"You're talking about your house here in Loon Lake, right?"

"Yes, honey, my home. You know my place. I still have the bedroom ready for the kids. . . ."

"Lorraine, I've not heard a thing about a dam going in

around here. Not in Loon Lake, not in Rhinelander, not in the county. When did this happen?"

"Last month. All they gave me was twenty thousand dollars."

"For Pete's sake, Lorraine, your property is worth five times that much. More even. *Much* more."

"That's what I thought but they told me I had just twenty-four hours to accept their offer or I'd get nothing. I know the county can do that, y'know. Condemn property and not pay you. Happened to my great-grandfather—"

"Lorraine, that was in the late 1800s when the railroad was being built. Not today and not on such short notice—but let me check into this. And who made the offer?"

"Two men from Brokers Real Estate Agency. One is named Tom. The other one is some rich fella with big hair. You know, a pomperanian."

"You mean a pompadour?"

"Yeah, like that."

"And Tom who?"

"That's all I know—Tom."

Geez Louise, thought Lew. "You have paperwork on all this, I hope?"

"They said they'd mail it, although I don't have it yet. But, see, now I hear there isn't going to be a dam. So they have my land. . . ."

"And all you have is twenty thousand dollars."

"Lewellyn . . ." Lorraine began to cry. "I should've called you before, shouldn't I."

"I wish you had but I'll look into this. Lorraine, can you come by the police department at ten tomorrow morning?

Bring any notes and paperwork that you might have. They gave you a bill of sale, right?"

"I'll check. I know I signed something but my memory isn't all that good these days. I can ask Gloria to help me."

Before getting off the phone, Lew made sure Lorraine had her personal cell number and jotted down the address of where the old woman was now living.

Wow, Lew thought after setting the phone back on its base, an elderly woman with memory problems sitting on a valuable piece of land: perfect target for an unscrupulous real estate investor. And "Brokers Real Estate Agency"? She had never heard of such a real estate company in the area. A quick search on her cell phone didn't turn one up either. Curious.

———

Driving back into town, Lew couldn't stop the flood of sad memories generated by the sound of Lorraine's voice. First was the death of Lew's son, Jamie. As vivid as if it were yesterday was the image of the seventeen-year-old lying dead in a tavern parking lot, victim of a knife wound during a bar fight. But the reality was that her son had been the victim of behavior patterns learned from Jimmy, his belligerent alcohol-fueled father.

Lew had fallen in love with Jimmy her senior year in high school. He was tall, cute, and fun. Two babies later she realized the source of the fun: alcohol. Too much alcohol. That plus his obvious lack of interest in holding down a job and helping her to build a life for their young family led to an ugly confrontation during which Jimmy got physical. Too physical for Lew. She filed for divorce.

A painful conversation with Lorraine followed. Lew would

never forget their final words to one another. "I don't understand, Lewellyn," Lorraine had said, "why are you leaving my Jimmy? He promised me he'll try to make a good living. . . ."

"Lorraine, he hit me."

"But, honey, his father hit me. You know it only happens when they're drinking. . . ."

"Once was enough," Lew had said, closing the door on Lorraine and her marriage. Though she took her son and daughter with her, they still visited their father. He was dead now, but Lew would always blame Jimmy, blame the kind of man he became as the drinking worsened, for their son's death.

She was pulling into the parking lot for the Loon Lake Police Department when her personal cell phone rang. It was Osborne.

"Lew, Chuck is dead."

CHAPTER SEVEN

Ten minutes later, standing alongside Osborne, Lew stared down at the still form that had been Chuck Pelletier. The body was sprawled facedown where he had fallen onto a worn braided rug, a sport coat bunched up around his neck, arms bent at the elbows, hands facing out. Just above Chuck's head, she could see a spattering of red droplets leaking into the rug.

To the right of the body, on the floor near a scarred coffee table holding a copy of Joan Wulff's *Fly Casting Techniques*, was an empty whiskey bottle. The whiskey must have spilled as the bottle rolled because the room reeked of alcohol.

"So . . . Chuck was drinking again?" she asked as she gazed around the room. She recognized fly-tying equipment on the large desk in one corner, and there were framed collections of trout flies interspersed with sculptural pieces of driftwood decorating the walls. A wooden rack in the far corner held four fly rods. Half a dozen reels were stored in a glass display case nearby.

"No," said Osborne, his voice hard. "Absolutely not. Hasn't had a drink in two years. Think about it, Lew. I talked to him less than two hours ago and the man was as sober as I am standing here." Lew could hear anger in his voice.

Lew nodded. "Okay, Doc, take it easy. Just saying what it might look like to a stranger walking in. . . ."

"What it looks like is someone thinks we're a bunch of goddamn local yokels," said Osborne, "someone who may have heard that Chuck had a history of alcoholism but doesn't realize what it means that he hasn't missed an AA meeting in two years. Not one. And certainly not the one we attended together last week.

"Plus I talked to the man less than two hours ago and he was stone cold sober. I doubt a raging alcoholic could get drunk enough to pass out in that short a time. . . ."

What Osborne didn't say was what he was thinking: given that people in their AA group were sworn to secrecy, there was only one person who could have shared Chuck's history of alcoholism, and that would be Patti.

"All right, I need to call our esteemed coroner, the not-always-sober Ed Pecore, ASAP, and then the Wausau boys," said Lew, referring to the Wausau Crime Lab, which she depended on whenever she had to investigate a death occurring under questionable circumstances. Whether an accident, a murder, or a felony assault, the resulting investigation would require manpower, equipment, and technical expertise that the Loon Lake Police Department could not afford.

"Then I'll need both my officers out here to help secure the crime scene," said Lew, talking more to herself than to Osborne.

Again Lew looked around, taking in the contents of the room before saying, "Should I assume this was kind of a hideout for your friend? Like the hideaway in your garage?" She gave a gentle smile as she spoke.

Osborne had shown her the small room attached to the porch where he cleaned fish—a porch his late wife, Mary Lee, refused to enter, insisting she could smell fish guts. That was fine with Osborne.

What she didn't know was that one wall of the porch, the wall holding dozens of his muskie lures, hid another room. That room was tucked behind a fake wall in his garage and was a safe haven where he could get away from Mary Lee's querulous badgering.

The room might be tiny but it was large enough to hold his old office chair on its ancient rollers and three tall oak file cabinets he had inherited from his father, who had also practiced dentistry. The cabinet drawers were packed with patient files from his thirty-year dental practice—files Mary Lee had insisted he trash.

But for Osborne, those files were more than paper records. They were memories of a profession he had loved, of patients he had known and helped. Maybe that was why he had felt so close to Chuck. It wasn't just the shared experience of conquering their addiction but because he, too, had needed a secret place to hide.

Lew was reaching for her official cell phone when Osborne touched her arm. "Would you mind if I took a closer look at Chuck's neck and head before you call Pecore?"

"I can wait a minute or two," said Lew, "then I'll hope that I can't reach that jabone. If he doesn't answer immediately, I'll deputize you to be Loon Lake's acting coroner, in which case you'll be *required* to check the body for signs of life. And you know how to avoid damaging any evidence that Bruce and the Wausau boys will need."

Osborne hurried to his car and grabbed the black bag holding the instruments needed for the practice of forensic dentistry. Back in the room, he pulled on nitrile gloves, thinking—as he had since he walked into the room and found his friend—that something looked odd. But he also knew he was operating strictly on gut feeling.

The body might be lying facedown, but years of dentistry had made Osborne an expert on the human skull both front and back. It helped, too, that in college before he had settled on following his father into dentistry, he had considered becoming a sculptor and had studied the shape of the human head extensively. (That was before his dad had warned him, "Paul, being a sculptor is a hard way to make a living.")

Osborne reached down and with a delicate nudge of his instrument he was able to get a closer look at one side of Chuck's forehead. And he knew. Or thought he did.

He looked up at Lew: "I see the early signs of an abrasion or a contusion—a slight, very slight change in skin coloration. The forensic pathologist with the crime lab will know better, but I suspect Chuck was blindsided with something harder than that whiskey bottle."

Once again Lew looked around the room. This time she paid attention to the six worn wooden stairs that led from the main floor of the barn down and into the room that Chuck had outfitted for his fly tying. It must have been a storage area back when the old barn housed dairy cows.

"Whoever did this wants us to think Chuck had been

drinking, fell down those steps, hit his head and . . ." Then she was quiet, thinking.

Osborne waited.

Lewellyn Ferris may not have gone to college, but she had had excellent training in law enforcement, she was as savvy about people as she was about the inhabitants of a trout stream, and, more important, she was confident in her own judgment. More than once, when he had been deputized to help with an investigation, he had been impressed with her logic and her willingness to take a chance on a personal hunch.

"Tell you what, Doc, let's keep this to ourselves until we have an official report from the pathologist. For right now, if the press gets wind of this, the word is we're investigating a fatal accident. If whoever is behind this wants us to think it was an accident, we'll go along with that. Encourage them to make another atrocious error."

"Lew, no matter how this looks to us right now," said Osborne, "I'm not sure he was killed *here*. What about in his car? Or outside this building? Or on his way here from his office?"

"The office. Good point," said Lew. "He may have met someone in the office and driven here—or run into someone on his way here? Who knows? But there could be evidence in his office. . . ."

She exhaled as the scope of the investigation dawned on her. "I better see if the Wausau boys can send more people and I'll have Dispatch reach the sheriff's office. It's going to take more manpower than myself and Officers Donovan and Adamczak to secure these sites."

Stepping outside to place her first call, Lew grimaced as Ed Pecore answered on the first ring. "Darn," she mouthed, looking over at Osborne. Taking care to mask her disappointment, she gave Pecore directions to the two-lane road leading to the barn. "There's no fire number on the county road, Ed," she said, "so keep your eyes peeled once you've passed the Pelletier driveway, which has a blue mailbox."

About to make more calls, she was alarmed to see Osborne leaning against his car with his arms crossed, a baleful expression on his face. "Dammit, Lew, I should have gone right to Chuck's office—not made all those foolish phone calls. . . ." He shook his head as he spoke.

"But how could you know this would happen?" asked Lew, hearing the despair in his voice.

"Maybe you're right," said Osborne. "But given what Chuck told me this morning . . ." Again he shook his head. "Gordon Maxwell and that goofy wife of Chuck's better have damn good alibis for the last two hours."

Lew decided to let that remark go, saying, "Excuse me, Doc, I've got Pecore on his way and I need to put in a call in to the Wausau boys—"

"Insist on Bruce Peters," said Osborne, interrupting. "He's the only one of those razzbonyas knows what the hell he's doing."

"All right, okay. Doc, I want you to take a deep breath," said Lew, placing a hand on Osborne's right arm. "I know this isn't easy but I don't want you jumping to conclusions, and I have to caution you against saying something that might jeopardize the investigation."

"I know, I know," said Osborne, removing her hand. "I'll

calm down. It's just"—his eyes glistened—"this is so . . . hard. If you knew what Chuck had been through . . ."

"You've told me, Doc, and I will do my best to get Bruce in on this. But right now it's critical that you not jump to conclusions on Maxwell. Could be he and Chuck were both set up."

While she was talking, Ed Pecore drove up in a battered Toyota Camry. Wheezing as he eased his overweight body out from under the steering wheel and swung his pudgy legs onto the ground, he managed to say, "Okay, Ferris, what's up?"

Osborne snorted at the intended rudeness: Pecore never failed to make it obvious he was allergic to addressing Lew by her correct title.

"Morning, Ed," said Lew in a brisk tone that ignored the insult. "Say, didn't I just see your car parked over at Three Pines Tavern? That's half a mile away." She glanced at her watch. "I called you fifteen minutes ago—what took so long?"

"Oh, you know, checkin' in with my buddy, Jack Oelrich. He's the fire marshal, y'know. I heard there was a grassfire over on Shepard Lake Road. . . ."

"Sure you weren't sampling his supply of Leinies?" asked Lew, referring to Wisconsin's homegrown beer. She relished needling the jerk.

Ed Pecore had been appointed to the position of Loon Lake coroner immediately after his brother-in-law, Phil Andrews, was elected mayor of Loon Lake. Until then he had owned a small tavern back on County Road MB, where it was rumored he spent his days overserved while sitting on his own barstools.

If the joke was that consuming alcohol was Wisconsin's "state sport," Ed Pecore was a leading scorer.

But that was no concern of the new mayor, who had been more interested in his sister, Pecore's wife, being able to count on the coroner position's annual salary and health benefits.

Lew would never forget what Phil had said when she questioned the appropriateness of appointing a bartender to be the town coroner: "Hey, Chief Ferris, if he can figure out a dead soldier [referring to an empty beer bottle], he can figure out if a body is living or dead, doncha know." And he had laughed off her suggestion that he choose a health professional for the position.

So Ed Pecore got the job and he would keep the job until Phil Andrews got divorced or lost the next election. Since Phil had been reelected twice to a position no one in their right mind wanted, Lew resigned herself to doing the best she could to manage the Loon Lake Police Department's files in spite of Pecore's talent for messing up the chain of custody for critical evidence on those occasions when he had to report a cause of death "due to unknown circumstances."

She also kept an eye on the conditions surrounding the reporting of a deceased individual, as Ed had the bad habit of bringing his two Dobermans with him when called in as coroner. More than once, when he had arrived to confirm a death, he had let the dogs follow him into the room where a body lay. Grieving relatives should not have to deal with dogs nuzzling their loved one even if it was, as Ed had said, "just a sniff or two. Didn't hurt a thing."

The only good news was that since Pecore was neither a medical examiner nor a pathologist, Lew could banish him to his favorite barstool whenever identification of a dead body was required. And turn to her best friend, Dr. Paul Osborne.

Theirs was a friendship forged in a trout stream on a summer night when Osborne, recently widowed, was under the impression he was going to have a lesson on casting a fly rod from a guy named "Lou." But "Lou" turned out to be "Lew"— not a guy at all.

And the lesson turned out to be about more than just casting a fly rod as Osborne discovered a woman who could laugh easily and with a warmth that surprised him. Lew was impressed, too. He might be awkward with a fly rod but he tried hard, did not condescend as men often do to women who fish—and, thanks to a stint in the military during his years in dental school, he turned out to be proficient in the field of dental forensics, a scientific interest he continued to follow even after his retirement.

Not even the Wausau boys in the crime lab an hour away from Loon Lake could boast of being able to afford having an odontologist on staff, so Lew was able to deputize Dr. Paul Osborne to help identify corpses. This was most helpful when Pecore was unavailable due to what his wife called an "indisposition" (known to locals familiar with Pecore as a "hangover").

In time Osborne's role as a deputy coroner had expanded when an investigation demanded more man-hours than Lew and her two officers could manage, including interrogations.

Thirty years practicing dentistry had also taught Osborne the rare skill of listening past the obvious ("Dr. Osborne, I feel a spot on my gum up here") to the subtle hints that a patient's problem might lie elsewhere than in their mouth; i.e., from hypochondria to the abuse of painkillers to symptoms of physical abuse and more.

Lew recognized early on that Osborne's listening skills were different from her own—so different that when conducting an interrogation together they made a valuable team.

But theirs was not a strictly professional relationship. It may have been the third lesson in the trout stream or it may have been the second time that Osborne helped with the identification of a body found decaying in a swamp (an Alzheimer's victim who had wandered off weeks earlier) that Lew became acutely aware that the widowed retired dentist might be sixty-three years old but he was damn good-looking for a man of that age. That was when she decided life was too short not to risk fooling around. After all, they were both adults.

And so today, two years into sharing a daily morning coffee in the office of the Loon Lake chief of police—and helping on investigations when needed—Osborne still couldn't believe his good luck.

———

"Whoa, stop right there, Ed," said Lew loudly as Pecore started toward the entrance to the barn. "Where are your shoe covers?"

"Whaddya talking about?" asked Pecore. "Trying to tell me this is a crime scene?"

"We don't know if it is or isn't." Lew shot Osborne a quick glance as she spoke. Pecore was famous for unloading the details of his professional duties at the nearest barstool on his way into town.

"But just in case, I have established an entry and exit path and I'll need you to stay within that with shoe covers on. And, puh-leeze do not touch anything. Keep the chain of custody clean this time. Got it?"

Pecore gave a grumpy shrug as he opened the trunk of his car for shoe covers. After Lew repeated her instructions on where to walk so that he wouldn't disturb or damage any trace evidence, Pecore followed them back into the barn and down the stairs into the room where Chuck Pelletier's body lay.

A few minutes earlier, while waiting for Pecore to slip on the paper slippers, Osborne had noticed that the coroner's eyes were bloodshot and he needed a Kleenex for what was happening to his nose. But Pecore, unconcerned with his symptoms, proceeded to lean down for a look at the body just as he let go with a hearty sneeze. Snot flew across the room.

"Out of the building, Ed," said Lew, sharply. "Now." She emphasized the word and stared at Pecore until he stepped back. "With that cold you could contaminate this entire crime scene."

"Why do you keep saying 'crime scene'?" asked Ed, wiping at his nose and mouth with the sleeve of his denim jacket. "Don't you smell the whiskey? Whoever this commode is, he prob'ly drank himself to death. That's what I'm putting on my coroner's report. No doubt about it. Not when the place smells to high heaven of booze."

"Ed," said Lew, pointing to the doorway as she spoke, "you put alcoholism down as 'cause of death' and I can assure you the City Council will hear from me. And don't you forget—they can overrule your brother-in-law. You want to keep your job? I suggest you inform me right now, officially, that you have a contagious head cold and need to be excused from your duties." Pecore's eyes widened in protest.

"Don't worry, Ed," said Lew with a wave of her hand. "You're on salary, so you'll still be paid. But if you will do that, then I can deputize Doc Osborne and have him complete the paperwork so I can turn the victim over to the Wausau Crime Lab."

Pecore looked at her in amazement. "*You're calling in the Wausau boys?* Jeez, Ferris, they cost money. I know this is no crime. You got a guy drank himself to death. I see it, I smell it."

Lew gave him the dim eye. "Need me to repeat what I just told you?"

"Okay, okay, I'm done here. But"—Pecore wagged a finger at Lew—"I'm going to tell Phil what you're doing."

"You do that, Ed. And you be sure to mention it took you fifteen minutes to get here because your damn car was parked at a tavern *half a mile away*."

Ed shrugged and walked toward the door, sneezing as he went. This time he put up an arm to block the sneezes.

CHAPTER EIGHT

Osborne pulled over a chair to sit beside Chuck's body while Lew made phone calls. Unreasonable though the feeling was, he didn't want to leave his friend alone. Plus someone had to stay with the body.

After he had completed filling out the coroner's report, he leaned down to give Chuck's still shoulder a reassuring pat as he said in a soft voice, "I hope you were hit from behind, friend. I hope you never saw it coming."

Meanwhile, standing outside the barn to get better cell service, Lew was able to reach the Dispatch operator. To her relief, a twenty-year veteran of the department was on duty. "Marlaine, please alert Officers Adamczack and Donovan that I need them to report to me at this location as soon as possible. I know Officer Donovan is off duty until later today, but please explain to him the following situation."

After giving a brief description of the questions surrounding Chuck Pelletier's death, along with the addresses of the Pelletier home, the barn, and Chuck Pelletier's office, she said, "Once you've reached my officers, please notify the sheriff's department that the Loon Lake Police have a fatality on the Pelletier property.

"Be sure to tell them that while the circumstances are uncertain at this time, I need their help securing the entire property, as it may turn out to be a crime scene. Ask them to meet me here at the barn and we'll determine who should be assigned to which site. Any questions?"

"Nope. Got it, Chief."

Debating whom to call next—Ray Pradt or the Wausau Crime Lab—Lew opted for Ray. She needed him at the barn with his cameras as soon as possible. And she was also curious as to what he may have seen on her property. He answered immediately.

"Yep, Chief, you've been . . . robbed."

"I know *that*. That's not why I called—"

"Yep . . . shot those photos and"—he let the word hang out there—"dang vehicle was a four-wheeler for sure with . . . a trailer."

"Ray, I'm calling for another reason."

"O-o-h yeah? Shoot."

Finally, thought Lew, exhaling in exasperation. Hurriedly she described the scene at the barn and the need for him to get there as soon as possible.

"You know the drill, Ray," she added, "I need photos of the victim and every detail of the room the body is in—as well as photos of the entry to the barn and the clearing in front of the barn."

"Not to worry, Chief. Sounds like you're pretty sure this wasn't an accident so don't worry—I'll get it all."

"As soon as possible, Ray, before anything changes that might damage trace evidence. Any questions?"

"Ah-h, yes, one," said Ray. He was quiet for a long moment. Then he said without lingering over a word, "The victim. Isn't he . . . ? Wasn't he Doc's good friend? Nice fella. What in the hell—?"

"No idea. Best-case scenario, Bruce Peters and his crew will be able to help me out, but until I know for sure—"

"Look, I've got my cameras in the truck. Be there in five. Oh, and, Chief, while I was out at your place a guy from the DNR drove up. Said you'd texted him about the birches on your back forty. He took a look and said to tell you looks to him like you're a victim of the same crowd's been working other locations up here."

———————

Off the phone with Ray, Lew called the Wausau Crime Lab. "Hello, Chief Ferris," said the secretary for the director of the crime lab, "I'm afraid Director Shultz can't take your call. He is out for three days—a family funeral. Is there anyone else you'd like to speak with?"

Holding her breath and hoping, Lew said, "Bruce Peters, please."

"Certainly. I'll put you through."

Within seconds an excited male voice was on the phone—so excited Lew could visualize Bruce's bushy black mustache bouncing up and down. "Chief Ferris! I was just going to give you a call. How the heck you doing? I hear they're going to be stocking twenty-two-pound brown trout up in your neck of the woods—"

"Whoa, slow down, Bruce," said Lew. "Brown trout, brook trout, rainbow trout—put that aside for the moment, please. Afraid I have what I believe to be the victim of a murder that occurred a couple hours ago. I could be wrong but I doubt it. I need someone from the crime lab up here ASAP. Can you swing that or do I have to call your acting director for an approval?"

"No, no, *I'm* the acting director. Sure, I can be up there right away but give me a few details."

Lew described the scene in the barn and the connection between Osborne and the dead man, though she decided to leave out the information that Chuck had shared with Osborne regarding Gordon Maxwell and Chuck Pelletier's wife until they could speak in private.

"The victim recently moved to Loon Lake," said Lew, "he was a senior executive—the CFO—for the NFR's Partridge Lodge, which means there may be serious media interest. I'm hoping to keep this quiet until we know for sure if this was an accident or . . . not."

"You mean that new fly-fishing place? The huge expensive private one?"

"That's the place. A multi-million-dollar development that's been under way up here for about nine months. The victim was the CFO."

Bruce whistled. "That's what I was gonna call you about, Chief. I heard about that place when my wife and I were visiting friends in Land O' Lakes last weekend."

"Well, you're about to find out a whole lot more about it," said Lew drily. "How soon can you get here?"

"Within the hour, maybe a few minutes longer. I can use the copter and bring a photographer and my medical examiner along. But, Chief Ferris, you've got to nail down the victim's office as a crime scene, too. We'll need his computers and phones and—"

"Got it going already, Bruce. We're securing this location where Doc found the body as you and I speak—and I've got help from the sheriff's department securing the victim's home and office. Once we've got that done, I'll get Dani, my IT guru, going on the computers and phones. You remember how good she is. Sound okay?"

"And Ray Pradt, too. Is he around to photograph the body and site before I get there? Do you have a murder weapon?"

"Ray is on his way. But, Bruce, Doc and I haven't a clue as to a murder weapon. Doc is guessing blunt force trauma but that's just a guess. So, no—no obvious murder weapon."

"Could be somewhere on the property up there. You say the victim is in a barn away from his home?"

"Right. On his property but not in the family home."

"Hey, Chief, I don't have to tell you that none of my people are as good in the woods as ol' crazy Ray. Can we put him to work searching around the place? I know this is a busy time for his guiding business. . . ."

Crazy Ray. That's what Bruce Peters had taken to calling the young fishing guide from the day they'd met two years earlier. Ray had shown up to help track a suspect across a swamp filled with bogs and "loon poop," which is what locals call the quicksand-like pits of swamp muck that can suffocate unsuspecting hunters and hikers who stumble into them. While Ray could boast of tracking skills rarely found in the northwoods, he hardly looked like a serious woodsman.

A long, lean six foot six, Ray had a unique approach to human movement: his body folding and unfolding in sections with knees appearing to enter a room seconds before his shoulders. The effect was such that Osborne swore his neighbor was genetically related to an accordion.

It didn't help that he capped off his lanky, limber physique with a beat-up fishing hat crowned with a large stuffed trout whose head and tail extended out over his ears. As Bruce liked to say: "What the heck do you call a man who wears a fish on his head?" "Crazy Ray" worked.

———

"I'll talk to Ray about searching the area," said Lew. "He'll be arriving here to shoot in and around the barn any minute. And he had time this morning to help me out on another case, so he might be available. Should I call St. Mary's Hospital and have their paramedics ready to remove the body once your medical examiner has completed his exam?"

"No, I'll send ours. We have to bring the victim down here for the autopsy anyway. Anything else you need right now?"

"Just your beautiful face, Bruce."

"And my fly rod?"

Lew chuckled. "And your fly rod."

———

It wasn't until after that flurry of phone calls that she realized she and Osborne better make their way to the Pelletier home before someone surprised Chuck's wife with a roadblock at the end of her driveway. She hurried into the barn to get Osborne.

He was sitting alongside Chuck when she entered. As he got to his feet, his coroner's report in hand, they heard an unexpected noise: the call of a loon.

CHAPTER NINE

The slow, haunting loon call was coming from across the room under the coffee table. "That has to be Chuck's phone. It must have flown out of his pocket as he fell," said Lew as she and Osborne scrambled in different directions for fresh pairs of nitrile gloves. Osborne got his on first but by then the phone was silent.

Lew reached for the phone and, clicking it on, saw a series of "missed" calls with the most recent being from someone named Molly. "Molly? Who's Molly?" she asked Osborne.

"One of his daughters. He's got two."

Lew put the phone on speaker, hit CALL BACK, and waited.

"Dad?" asked a woman's voice, sounding petulant. "Where have you been? I tried you three times this morning."

"Molly—" Before Lew could say more, she was interrupted.

"Who is this? Is something wrong? Is my dad there?"

"Molly, this is Chief Lewellyn Ferris with the Loon Lake Police. Yes, something is very wrong."

"*What?* Is my dad okay?"

Lew took a deep breath, threw a quick glance at Osborne, and said, "I'm afraid your father is . . . he has passed away. I'm here with Dr. Paul Osborne, who found him. We're not sure of the circumstances, but we'll know soon enough." She paused for a moment. "Where are you calling from?"

"Evanston. I live here and I was just getting packed to come up for a visit with my dad . . . he was . . . he was fine when we talked yesterday. What on earth? How did he die?"

Her voice had gone flat, as people's voices do when confronted with unexpected, devastating news.

"We don't know yet—"

"A car accident? Where are you? Where is my dad right now?"

"We're in the barn at the back of your father's property—"

"You mean that room where he hides all his fly-fishing stuff? He loves being in there. Maybe he had a heart attack?"

Osborne motioned for Lew to hand him the phone.

"Molly? This is Paul Osborne, a good friend of your father's up here."

"Yes, he's told me about you. I know you were close. Were you with him when—" She couldn't finish.

"No. But I saw him earlier this morning and we'll talk when you get up here. But you need to know that we just found your father and we haven't had a chance to let your stepmother know what has happened. So please wait until we do.

"After Chief Ferris gives her the news, one of us will call you right back. And, Molly, I am so sorry but this just happened. . . ."

"Sure, sure, I understand, but I have to tell Jessie—my sister. So . . . um . . . when can I tell her?" A sharp breath as she held back a sob. Osborne could hear the young woman swallowing hard.

"As soon as we call you back. Shouldn't be long."

"Okay, but I'm going to throw some things in my bag and fly up there right now."

"Of course," said Lew, taking the phone back. "I'll arrange rooms at the Loon Lake Motel for you and your family—"

"If you mean Patti, don't call *that woman* 'my family,'" said Molly. As she spit out the two words, Osborne caught Lew's eye: they got that message loud and clear.

"Fine. I'll arrange to have separate rooms, in that case, for each of you."

"And my sister. She and I can stay together, but, Chief Ferris, why can't we just stay at my dad's place? Jessie and I have bedrooms there. . . ."

"I'm afraid the house will be off-limits until the crime lab forensics team has completed—"

"*What?* My father was murdered? Oh, my God—"

"Look, Molly," said Lew, "we'll talk more when I call you back. In just a few minutes. Stay by your phone. Okay?"

Molly gave a strangled "okay" before Lew ended the call.

———————

A minute later, she walked out to her cruiser where she reached into the trunk for a paper evidence bag. She was slipping the phone into the bag when Ray Pradt's battered blue fishing truck came rumbling up the two-lane road to the barn, the brass walleye mounted on the hood glinting in the sun.

Lew gave a nod to Osborne. "All right, Doc," she said, her voice grim, "with Ray here to stay with the body—time to see Mrs. Pelletier. Let me give him instructions and we can go."

Five minutes later, as Osborne was opening the door on the passenger side of Lew's cruiser, Lew saw the expression on his face and said, "Maybe I should handle this alone, Doc. This has to be hard for you."

"No," he said firmly, "I want to see how Patti reacts. After everything Chuck told me, I am curious to see. . . ."

Lew was silent as they drove to the house. Though she had offered to notify the widow by herself, she was relieved to have Osborne along. Given his close friendship with the woman's husband, especially his knowledge of Chuck's grief over the loss of his first wife and their shared battle with alcoholism, he was likely to pick up on nuances in Patti Pelletier's behavior that she might miss.

"Mrs. Pelletier?" Lew asked the slight, thin woman who appeared behind the screen door.

"Yeah," said the woman, "why?"

She made no move to open the door. Through the screen door Lew could see she was wearing tight-fitting flowered shorts and a pink top with a scoop neck edged in frills that exposed an overtanned breastbone. The shirt was stretched tight over not-so-subtle hints of full breasts. Lew could tell the woman thought she looked sexy—but it was "scrawny with fake boobs" that popped into Lew's mind.

"Mrs. Pelletier, I'm Chief Lewellyn Ferris with the Loon Lake Police Department. Dr. Paul Osborne is here with me—I believe you know him—and we need to talk to you. May we come in?"

"What? No, sorry, of course. Come in." Patti stepped back as Lew opened the screen door. She stared at Osborne, black-lined eyes questioning with no hint of coyness this time.

Standing in the foyer, Lew delivered the news gently, saying only that Osborne had found her husband dead in the barn. She added that since he did not appear to have died a natural death ("though we cannot be positive about that until after the autopsy"), the house and the barn would have to be immediately vacated until the Wausau Crime Lab's forensic team could conduct a search of the premises.

"What do you mean he didn't die a natural death? What exactly does that mean?"

"Only that how he died is not obvious. Until we know if there was an accident or some other cause, there has to be an investigation and an autopsy. That's why we need you to leave your house immediately."

Patti looked stunned. As if refusing to believe what Lew had just told her, she shook her head several times before asking, "You mean *me*? I have to leave my house? *Now*?"

Osborne couldn't tell what upset her more: the news of Chuck's death or that she had to get out of the house.

"I'll watch while you pack an overnight bag," said Lew. "Then I'll arrange for you and Chuck's daughters to stay in town."

"Wait, may I sit down for a minute?" Patti reached a trembling hand for a nearby straight-backed chair. "I just . . . I need to think about this."

"Certainly." Lew motioned to Osborne and said, "Dr. Osborne will stay with you while I step outside to make two phone calls. Take your time, Mrs. Pelletier. We know this is a shock.

"Just so you know, the first call I'm making is to Molly Pelletier, your stepdaughter. She happened to call on your husband's phone shortly after we found him. That's how she knows about his death. And now that we've informed you, I need to let her know that she can notify her sister.

"Do you want to talk to her when I'm finished?"

Patti shook her head no.

———————

After Lew left the foyer and was standing out on the walkway leading up to the front door, Patti looked up at Osborne and said in a small voice, "What am I going to do, Paul? I have no money."

"That doesn't make sense, Patti," said Osborne. "Chuck has been making a very good living—"

"But we haven't finished making our wills. I don't have anything of my own. This wasn't supposed to happen. . . ." She paused. Osborne said nothing. He wondered if she had stopped short of saying "yet."

CHAPTER TEN

Bruce Peters arrived at the barn within an hour, along with a photographer from the crime lab. They were accompanied by the medical examiner, a tall, cheerful woman in her early thirties, who introduced herself right away to Lew and Osborne. "Hi, I'm Eloise Sanderson," she said, "but you can call me Ellie." She stuck her hand out.

Before they could say a word in return, she said, "If you don't mind, I'll get right down to work, as I have our van arriving pretty darn soon to take the body down to Wausau for the autopsy."

With that she knelt down to open the red Craftsman toolbox she had carried into the barn. Peering over her shoulder, Osborne was impressed with the contents, which were quite different from the dental instruments he carried in his black bag.

Ellie saw him studying the assortment of knives, scalpels, forceps, and scissors. She chuckled. "I see your surprise, Dr. Osborne," she said, "but I'm trained to work on 'decomps'—victims who are in much further stages of decomposition than our friend here. You know, like the hunter who has a heart attack in the woods and can't be found for days because he left his phone in his truck? That's my specialty." She gave Osborne a wide smile.

"Ah, Ellie, just so you know, this man was a friend of mine," said Osborne, trying to sound matter-of-fact as she started to work on Chuck's body. "A very dear friend." With some difficulty, he resisted the urge to ask her to be gentle.

"Then perhaps you should leave the room," said Ellie, her voice kind. She sat back on her heels and waited for him to answer.

"Yes, I think I should," said Osborne. "But will you let me know right away once you know what caused his death?"

Ellie looked over at Lew, who nodded that that would be okay. "Dr. Osborne is deputized to help me with this investigation," she said. "I have only two officers and an IT person part-time. Dr. Osborne is our acting coroner and he will assist in other areas of the investigation, including interrogations. He understands the chain of custody better than Loon Lake's appointed coroner."

"But if he knew the victim?" Ellie asked.

"Eloise, everyone in Loon Lake knows everyone," said Lew.

———————

Within an hour of the arrival of Bruce Peters and his crew, Lew's officers, along with two sheriff's deputies, had been able to secure the house, the barn, and Chuck's office with only one wrinkle.

"I've been stopped by Mr. Pelletier's secretary and told I can't enter his office even though I have a warrant to do so," said Officer Adamczak by phone to Lew. "She wants me to call the CEO for permission."

"You know that's not necessary," said Lew, stepping outside the barn to stand near Osborne who was waiting by his car, "but put her on the phone. I'll explain the situation."

"Hello, Chief Ferris, this is Marion Hunter, Mr. Pelletier's secretary. . . ."

Chuck's secretary was very quiet once Lew informed her of his death and the legality of the warrant to establish the office as a crime scene. She went on to say that Dani Wright, an IT specialist also with the Loon Lake Police, would arrive shortly to pack up any computers used by Chuck Pelletier for transport back to the station for further investigation.

"Are you copied on his e-mails?" Lew asked the woman.

"No, only what he forwards to me. Do you want my computer?"

"We may, eventually, but not at the moment."

"Shouldn't you talk to Mr. Maxwell, too?" she asked after a long moment. "He's our boss. . . ."

"Is he next of kin to Mr. Pelletier?"

"No."

"Well, then he can hear the news when I'm ready to share it with the public. By the way, where is Gordon Maxwell? Is he nearby? Officer Adamczak said you are the only person in the office at the moment."

"Mr. Maxwell is in Las Vegas. Flew out there on his private plane late this morning."

"What time exactly?"

"I'm not sure. He just said he was leaving to meet in Las Vegas with two investors from Chicago and he would be back sometime tomorrow. Chief Ferris, thank you for discussing this with me. I feel much better letting Officer Adamczak take care of things here. Please let me know what else I can do to help."

She hesitated before managing to say through soft gulps, "Mr. Pelletier . . . he was a special, kind person. I am . . ." She broke into tears.

Lew finished the call and clicked off her phone with a heavy sigh. "Oh, Roger, Roger, Roger," she said, "how is it you've been on the force for seven years and you still don't know the protocol for securing a crime scene?" She threw Osborne a despairing look.

———

Lew knew as she ended the call with the secretary that she better check back later to make sure Officer Adamczak had followed through correctly. She had learned the hard way that the former life insurance agent was not real swift when it came to details.

Roger Adamczak had started out as an insurance agent only to find that he lacked the instincts of a good salesman. So he joined the Loon Lake Police thinking that writing up traffic summonses and handing out parking tickets would make for an easy route to a decent pension.

What he hadn't figured on was what life would be like under a no-nonsense chief of police like Lewellyn Ferris, a woman determined to let no drug deal or attempted robbery go unpunished. Investigations in Loon Lake had ramped up 100 percent after she took over—especially during the summer months, when miscreants from the cities thought a small town in northern Wisconsin an easy mark.

Poor Roger. He could count on one hand the number of days he'd been able to hand out parking tickets.

———

A few minutes after speaking to the secretary, Lew had another thought and called her back. "Marion, did Mr. Pelletier have any visitors this morning?"

"No. He arrived a little late but in time for his conference call with New York, I mean with the executives with the hedge fund who own NFR and the Partridge Lodge development. That call lasted over two hours. I know he was busy in his office and made one other brief call before leaving the office. Otherwise, I'm sure he left the building then because I saw him head to the garage, where he keeps his car."

"What about phone calls coming in?"

"None that I'm aware of, but he does have a cell phone and, with his office door closed, I wouldn't know if he'd gotten any calls on that phone."

"Thank you, Marion. I'm sure I'll have more questions. Is there a home number or cell phone where you can be reached? And I want you to have my private cell number, too—in case you remember anything."

"Chief Ferris, this is not sounding good," said Marion. "Are you trying to tell me someone *killed* Mr. Pelletier?"

"I'm not sure yet," said Lew, "but it's possible. Please keep that confidential until we know more."

"Of course."

———

Lew walked into the barn where Ellie was still examining the corpse. "Any news?" she asked.

"This man did not hurt himself falling. He was hit hard, very hard on the side of the head. Possibly twice, but the autopsy will tell us more."

"Do you think it happened here?"

"That's Bruce's territory. I just work with the body."

Lew returned to Osborne who was outside, leaning against his car with his arms crossed and head down, thinking hard. "Doc, Ellie said Chuck was struck on the side of the head at least once with enough force to cause his death. She won't know more until after the autopsy." Osborne nodded without saying anything.

Lew waited then said, "Doc, you haven't had anything to eat all day. You don't look good. I think you should go home. I'll stop by later when things have quieted down here."

"No," said Osborne with a slow shake of his head, "I appreciate your offer to stop by, Lew, but I need some time alone to think all this over. I'll see you in the morning." He walked around his car, climbed in, and drove off.

Watching his car down the drive, Lew knew the ache in his heart. If only she could do something but . . . She turned to walk back into the barn.

Once he got home, Osborne busied himself in the house. He fed the dog, he made a liver sausage sandwich—of which he ate half—then loaded his plate and cutting board into the dishwasher and, flattening his hands on the kitchen counter as he leaned forward, he stood staring down. He felt like he was avoiding himself.

A low rumbling caused him to glance out the window. Ray's pickup was going by. He decided to walk next door to his neighbor's trailer home—the one that had driven Osborne's late wife nuts. She used to complain about it all the time. "Paul, that awful place ruins, just *ruins* our view from the deck," she said at least several times a week. "Call the county again and demand that awful thing be condemned." Funny how Osborne kept forgetting to make that call. And now it didn't much matter. He sighed.

———————

Since her death, Osborne had found Ray's place a welcome sight, especially since Osborne and Charles had a pact: in an effort to control the still-frequent if unwelcome urge for alcohol, they mutually agreed that when either felt that urge, to signal it was time for a chat. Nothing more than a chat until the treacherous urge passed.

Often they met in Ray's comfortable kitchen with its view of Osborne's pristine, architecturally designed white frame lake house that had been built to Mary Lee's specifications (and approved by her bridge club). Osborne didn't mind the house—it had bedrooms for his grandchildren to sleep over—but he would have been just as happy in one of the small log cabins that hugged the lakeshore.

———————

As he crossed the clearing to Ray's front door, which was tucked into the gaping jaws of a muskie, Osborne knew he was in bad humor. Not even the sight of the lurid, neon-green fish that Ray had painted across the front of his trailer could prompt his usual wry grin.

"Yo, Doc, *entre vous*," said the familiar voice from inside the trailer. "You are as welcome as . . . the flowers. Coffee?"

Ray was speaking so fast as he poured a cup of coffee that Osborne knew something was wrong before he could even think to reply.

"I am so pissed. I am so . . . so furious." Ray waved an angry hand as he set the coffeepot back on its stand. "Doc, you won't believe what has happened—*they followed me*!"

"Who, what?" asked Osborne. He was so taken aback by Ray's obvious distress that he forgot his own despair for a moment.

"Yeah, goddamn goombahs. Three boats of 'em—from Milwaukee. They watched me guiding a client last week and now, these last two days, they've been crowding my spots. I was out before six this morning and there they were. Big, fat, and ugly as turkey vultures.

"Doc, isn't there a law against stealing someone's fishing hole?" Osborne had never seen Ray's eyes so wide and angry.

"Don't think so," said Osborne. "No law on the books, at least as far as I know. But it is a matter of principle if not common courtesy not to crowd another fisherman's boat."

Shaking his head with anger, Ray directed his attention back to the sink, where he was rinsing off a good-size bluegill. "Where did you catch that?" asked Osborne as he admired the fish.

"Off my goddamn dock," said Ray in a mutter. "I'm not going out in my boat until those jerks get off my goddamn lake." He threw the poor fish onto a sheet of paper towel he'd spread on the drain board. "Hey, Doc—you're not listening to me. What the hell am I going to do about—"

Before he could finish, Osborne came unglued. His shoulders shook as he dropped his head, croaking, "Don't talk to me about *doing*. I'm the one should have done something. Me. If I had made Chuck come with me this morning he wouldn't be dead."

Ray stared at him, then walked over to the kitchen table and sat down. He motioned for Osborne to take the chair across from him. "What are you saying? What is this all about? I know he was a good friend and I'm sure you're upset, but I'm also sure that what has happened is no fault of yours."

And with that, Osborne spilled Chuck's story of Gordon Maxwell and Patti Pelletier trying to run him down in the driveway early that morning. How Chuck had driven to Osborne's immediately afterward to tell him what had happened only to resist Osborne's insistence he go with him to the police immediately.

"He said he had an important conference call and then he would meet with Lew . . . Ray, *I shouldn't have let him go to that office*," said Osborne, eyes glistening. "I shouldn't have let him go." He pounded the table with one fist as he spoke. Then he dropped his head and covered his face with his hands.

Ray was silent. After a few moments, Osborne looked up. He saw the concern in Ray's eyes and said, "If there is one thing in life I have learned, it is that friends like Chuck Pelletier are hard to find . . . you're one, Ray. You are one. Thank you for listening."

"Sorry for my rant," said Ray. "I didn't realize. . . ."

"Of course not. How could you have known?"

The younger man reached across the table to grasp Osborne's hands, which he was holding, fingers clenched, on top of the table in front of him. "What can I do to help?"

Osborne thought hard, then took a deep breath. "Maybe I can do one thing right today. One thing that might help. Up for a boat trip?"

"Right now?"

"Right now."

At the thought of what had just popped into his head, Osborne shifted in his chair, heart lifting for the first time in hours. "What if I show you my secret muskie hole—where the *really* big girls are? The spot my dad took me to years ago and where his father took him. I've never told you—"

"You aren't supposed to," said Ray with a gentle smile. "You know the rule: a fisherman should never share—"

"Forget that. You got these creeps usurping your best fishing spots? We'll show them. Plus life is too short. I've shared this with only two other people in my life—my daughter, Erin, and her daughter, Mason. If he behaves, I may share it with my grandson, Cody, too. But those are the only people who know my secret . . . and now you. But only so long as you promise to keep the secret, Ray."

"Can I take clients? You know, special clients?"

"Only if you kill them afterward. No, you may, of course, but be judicious. Only out-of-towners without the know-how to find their way back another day."

"Agreed."

And with that they shook hands, Ray grabbed the key for his inboard, and they ambled down to the dock in the late afternoon sun.

CHAPTER ELEVEN

Throttling down, Ray raised the boat's propeller to maneuver through the buoys in the channel from Loon Lake to Mirror Lake. After passing over the shallow flats and avoiding the boulders lurking beneath the surface of the channel, he sped across the lake to the channel leading from Mirror Lake to Silver Bass Lake.

Again the outboard's propeller came up and Ray guided the boat through buoys and across Silver Bass until they reached a final set of buoys marking the entrance to the Loon River. "How far, Doc?" asked Ray.

"Not far," said Osborne, welcoming the sense of peace he felt every time he reached the river on his way up the Loon Chain. For him, a trip up the river was a trip into the past, a journey with ghosts: he had first fished here with his grandfather, then his father, then many close friends, some of whom were gone. One of those friends was Chuck Pelletier.

Much as Chuck favored fly-fishing for trout, he had indulged Osborne when Osborne insisted on taking him up the chain of lakes and especially the Loon River. It was home to the great blue heron and an ancient eagles' nest that had survived decades of winter blizzards and summer tornadoes, and still served as home for eaglets and their extended family. And home, too, to turtles—lots and lots of turtles. But not even Chuck had been shown what he was about to share with Ray.

I guess I'm feeling mortal today, thought Osborne, as he raised his right hand to alert Ray to slow down. "As we enter this bay," he shouted over the roar of the outboard motor, "head for the north end and slow way, way down."

Ray nodded and did as he was told. The motor died and the fishing boat drifted into a wider expanse of water. "Great temp tonight," said Ray, glancing around him. "Love fishing when it's in the upper seventies this time of the year. Great for action, don't y'know." He looked back at Osborne who was sitting near the bow of the boat. He waited for instruction.

"All right," said Doc, "you can't see down through this dark water but we're over the only forty-foot hole along the entire chain. My grandfather told me years ago that it's fed by a cold underwater spring that the big muskies—you know, the forty- to fifty-inch big girls—love. He got a fifty-five-incher here one year. I didn't see it, my old man told me about it. There's a deep weed bed here that draws 'em in."

Ray scanned the shoreline, noting the patterns in the tamaracks crowding one another in the wetlands: along with the outline of the treetops against the sky, he committed to memory the bleached skeletons of two fallen tamaracks and a mound of boulders on the shore. He would need those images to find this place again. That would be a challenge, as the Loon River wound through the wetlands for nearly two miles with every turn looking identical to the one before and the one after.

Reading his mind, Osborne said, "Two minutes at medium speed past that eagles' nest."

"Going for suspended muskie here?" asked Ray as he moved to get his muskie rod and open his tackle box.

"Yep, I'd use a surface mud puppy if I were you. I like yellow or white—nice and bright on stained water."

Ray nodded. "Yeah, you might be right, Doc. But I'm going for my bucktail. I'll let it skitter along on the top of the water like surface bait though. Lately I've had luck with bucktails. I think they look natural and that seems to be working for me right now."

It wasn't until he stood to cast that Ray noticed Osborne hadn't moved. "What? Aren't you going to fish?"

"Not sure. Do you mind? I'm happy just watching. It's been a long day." Ray gave him a look of understanding before reaching his rod back and forward, the bucktail arcing high and far into the evening air.

Osborne looked around him, pleased to be out on the water, pleased to be in the company of someone for whom he could do something good. He knew the fishing hole would prove priceless for his friend: Ray might not catch any fish tonight, but he would soon, and when he did, the muskie would be a trophy.

The sun lazed its way toward the horizon, turning the sky into a fog of molten gold: soft, iridescent, enveloping. Osborne had a sense of Chuck being nearby; Chuck, who, like himself, had loved being close to water.

Ray's boat rocked gently on ripples and all Osborne could think was that sometimes a day comes along that unpredictably punctuates the story of your life. It had been that kind of day.

He had no need to fish.

CHAPTER TWELVE

The next morning Lew was in her office by 5:00 a.m., hoping to complete some of the paperwork generated by the death of Chuck Pelletier. To her relief, the pathologist for the Wausau Crime Lab had conducted the autopsy late the evening before and confirmed the medical examiner's opinion. The e-mail she had received shortly after midnight made the conclusion all too clear. *The victim*, it read, *an adult male, died of two episodes of blunt force trauma. . . .*

She waited until six thirty before waking Bruce up in his room at the Loon Lake Motel. "I got the same e-mail, Chief," he said. "You need a statement for the press?"

"Yes, and any chance we could have a brief press conference by eight thirty? I have a meeting at ten that I can't miss. Oh, and Dispatch told me that Chuck Pelletier's oldest daughter, Molly, checked into the motel last night, too. I'm hoping to connect with her and meet with her around eleven this morning out at Pelletier's barn. She told Dispatch she wants to see where her father died and I understand that.

"You'll want to be there, of course, and I'll include Doc, too. He's a good listener and we may learn something from the daughter."

"Is that the only family besides the wife?" asked Bruce.

"No, one more daughter, who is probably arriving today."

"What about Pelletier's boss? This Maxwell guy? After what you and Doc told me about Chuck thinking that Maxwell and the wife tried to run him over, I'd be interested in what he has to say."

"That makes three of us," said Lew. "I talked to Pelletier's secretary late yesterday afternoon after she'd told me Maxwell was in Las Vegas with investors. Apparently he flies there regularly on a private plane. She said she called him about Chuck's death and he said he would fly back immediately. We should be able to catch up with him today, too.

"Okay, Bruce, you can go back to sleep now."

"Oh sure, thank you. See you at eight thirty—in front of the courthouse, right?"

The press conference with three reporters—one each for the newspapers and local shopper covering Loon Lake but based in Rhinelander, as well as a young woman from the Rhinelander television station—went smoothly.

Immediately after introducing herself and Bruce, Lew deferred to Bruce, who emphasized that the investigation was ongoing. He explained that the only information currently available was the news that an executive from the Northern Forest Resorts development group had died unexpectedly. "There'll be more information to come once the official results are in," he added.

Lew clapped Bruce on the shoulder afterward. "You

Wausau boys know how to handle the press. But more important, I'm pleased you didn't say too much."

"I'm not stupid," said Bruce, "except when it comes to matching the hatch in the trout stream." He grinned. "I know today will be crazy but maybe we can fish tomorrow?"

"Let's hope," said Lew, checking her watch. "Oh, excuse me, I've got a meeting. I'll catch up with you and everyone out at the Pelletier barn in an hour."

———

Lorraine arrived five minutes early. Lew walked out to greet her and was surprised to find her alone. "I thought your friend, Gloria, was bringing you," she said to the woman whom she hadn't seen in nearly twenty years.

"She had to take her dog to the vet," said Lorraine. "She'll be back to pick me up. Lewellyn, thank you so much for taking the time to help me with this."

Lew waved away her gratitude. "It's my job. Come on, this way to my office."

"You know you haven't changed," said Lorraine, "you are still so strong. Just like always—you make things happen."

"For heaven's sake, Lorraine, you are giving me way more credit than I deserve and I am not sure that I can help you. So, please, sit down and show me what you found."

After the elderly woman had settled into one of the chairs in front of her desk, Lew said, "I'm hoping you've got more information on the sale of your home and the men who bought it. Do you?"

———

Over the nearly twenty years since Lew had last seen her, Lorraine had put on so much weight that Lew might not have recognized her. The voice had not changed, however, and hearing her brought back—just as it had a day earlier when she heard the message on the old landline telephone—a memory flash of her son's death. A flash of sadness and the anger she still felt toward her late, former husband whose bad behaviors had started to manifest themselves in the eighteen-year-old.

But was it really fair to blame Jamie's father? Lew had to admit he was not solely at fault. She was still angry with herself for what she might have done differently—if only she had known what to do.

She would never forget the last time she had seen Lorraine before today: it was the day her divorce was final and she had stopped to say goodbye to the mother-in-law who had always treated her with kindness. As she left Lorraine's house that day, she was aware that all she had in the world was twenty-six dollars, two kids, and a dog. Oh, and a job as a secretary at the mill for which she had just been hired. But that was then.

No regrets.

Pushing aside the memories, Lew forced herself to focus on Lorraine's words.

". . . So I couldn't find their names," the woman was saying, "but I found this." She was reaching into her purse when there was a tentative knock on the door before it was eased open. Osborne stood in the doorway, a questioning look on his face. This was the time each day when he would stop in for one last cup of coffee after an hour of coffee with his buddies at McDonald's.

"Too busy today, Chief?" he asked from the doorway.

"Come on in, Doc," said Lew. She introduced him to Lorraine and said, "Dr. Osborne is helping us with another investigation, but he knows so many people in Loon Lake that let's tell him what happened to you, in case someone he knows might be able to help."

Lorraine had pulled a newspaper photo from her purse and held it in her lap for the few moments it took her to explain to Osborne where her property was and how the two men had pressured her to sell for so little money or risk having it condemned.

Osborne listened and then said, "It's interesting that they approached you to sell. Sounds like your land abuts the NFR development—"

"What's that?" asked Lorraine.

"The Northern Forest Resorts development—the area where the Partridge Lodge Fishing and Hunting Preserve is being built. I wonder if they aren't thinking they can sell your land at a nice profit to that group. Boy oh boy, too bad you don't have the names of those two real estate agents. Are you sure you don't have documentation of your sale?"

Lew signaled him with her eyes. She would let him know later that Lorraine, who had to be over eighty years old, was not only forgetful but also might have more serious cognitive memory problems. "Lorraine has a good friend who is helping her go through papers and things, Doc," she said.

"Oh, but I do have this." Lorraine held out a photo from the local shopper. "I found this yesterday when my friend and I were clipping coupons—that's one of the men. The man on the right."

She handed the photo across the desk to Lew. Osborne walked around to look over Lew's shoulder. The photo was of two men standing side by side at a Rotary luncheon. Lew studied the photo, then shook her head. "Not familiar to me. You know him, Doc?"

Even though the page of newsprint was creased through the center of the photo, Osborne had no difficulty recognizing the guy in the business suit. Standing much shorter than the man to his left, the individual who bought Lorraine's land had a distinct appearance: he had a head full of dark wavy hair that appeared to stand a good three inches straight up from his forehead. And, if Osborne had to guess based on the one time they had met, it was fixed in place with a spray of concrete-strength mousse.

The hair was the defining feature as the eyes were dark and close set and the nose and chin firm in a bland Caucasian sort of way. Although his petite size also made him memorable—at least enough that one of Osborne's McDonald's buddies, who had met the man at a Chamber of Commerce meeting honoring the presidents and CEOs of local firms, had chortled over coffee the next morning: "I couldn't believe the guy—he wears lifts in the heels of his shoes. Kid you not."

Osborne looked up from the photo. "I know the man," he said, "I've seen him once. We met about two months ago. I was picking Chuck up at his office for an evening of fly fishing and Chuck introduced us—that's Gordon Maxwell."

CHAPTER THIRTEEN

Are you thinking what I'm thinking?" Osborne asked Lew after Lorraine had left.

"Need to know more about our friend Maxwell," said Lew. "Did you recognize the man in the photo with him?"

"No, but that could have been a candid photo shot at the luncheon, with those two having no connection other than standing in line at the salad bar. Let's make a copy of that photo and I'll show it to my friend Herm. He's in Rotary, he'll know."

"Are you feeling better, Doc?" asked Lew with a touch on his elbow.

Osborne tried to grin. "A little. I do realize Chuck was bound and determined to handle that conference call, but that's the last time I act against my better judgment. So don't try any funny stuff, Lewellyn." Again the attempt at a grin.

"You're a good man, Doc," said Lew, buckling on her gun, walkie-talkie, and cell phone. "Let's go meet the daughter. She wants to see where her father died."

As Osborne pulled his Subaru up next to Lew's cruiser, he saw a young woman standing with Bruce near the entrance to the barn. Also, off to one side, was Patti Pelletier. She appeared to be watching as Bruce was explaining something to the young woman.

On seeing Osborne get out of his car, the young woman walked toward him, her arms out. Without a word she embraced him, then stood back and said, "I'm Molly Pelletier, Dr. Osborne. My dad told me so much about you. You really helped him, you know?" She wiped away tears. "He needed a friend and you were someone he could trust. Thank you."

"I am so sorry—"

"S-h-h-h, no more," she said. "Dad's gone and what I have to do now is find out why. Mr. Peters was just filling me in on how Dad died. Now I want to see where." Shoulders back, Molly turned to Bruce, who had been waiting. "Show me the entry and exit route again, please?"

"Me, too," said Patti from where she was standing off to the right.

"No," said Molly, turning on her. "You stay far away from me—and from Jessie. We want nothing to do with you. Understand?"

"But . . . the funeral?" Patti's voice faltered.

"I'm handling it. You keep your goddamn nose out."

"But, legally . . ." Patti's voice was growing fainter with each word.

"He's my father and if you get in the way, I'll see that you get nothing out of his will. It was never signed, you know. I checked. He's never made a will at all; he never felt he had to when he was married to our mother."

Osborne wasn't completely convinced that she was right about that—it seemed odd to him that Chuck had never thought about such things when his kids were young—but her words certainly had the desired effect. With a stricken look on her face, Patti leaned back against the barn. She made no move to follow Molly, Lew, and Bruce Peters into the barn.

Entering the barn after the others, Osborne was impressed with Molly's strength. It wasn't just that she was so well spoken but she looked strong, too. She was of medium height and sturdy with solid bone structure and the muscles of an athlete—a hockey player perhaps? Maybe soccer. She reminded him of Lew: a woman who carried weight but not fat; a face open, honest, attractive but not pretty, at least not in a traditional way; and a voice that echoed authority.

Molly gazed down at the diagram that outlined where her father had fallen. She looked around the room. "Something's missing," she said.

Bruce and Lew looked at her quizzically. "See that empty hook on the wall there?" She pointed to a hook in the midst of a display of unusual pieces of driftwood. "Dad collected driftwood from all over and one we found together one year when we were sailing on Chesapeake Bay is gone. That's odd."

"Maybe your stepmother knows—"

"No. She was never allowed in here."

"Isn't *that* rather odd?" asked Lew.

Concerned that Patti was standing right outside the barn, Molly lowered her voice. "My dad was so lonely after my mother died that he married too soon. You know, he and Patti have only been married about a year and a half. Right after they moved here, he called me. He said he had made a mistake, but it wasn't her fault.

"You have to know that my parents loved to fly-fish together. Dad had so many wonderful memories from those days and he decided to make this room his way to spend time with my mom. Sad, I know, but I like to think those hours made him happy."

"What did the piece of driftwood look like? Maybe it's around here somewhere," said Bruce.

"It looks like a cane—a long, smooth piece of wood with a round knob on one end. Dad and I thought it looked like the leg bone of some prehistoric monster," said Molly with a laugh. "It's old-growth wood that is waterlogged and heavy as a rock—so tough you can't even carve on it."

As they walked out of the barn, Molly asked Lew, "When do you think the crime lab will return Dad's body? My sister and I need to make arrangements for him to be cremated."

"Tomorrow," said Bruce before Lew could answer. "I talked with our pathologist and forensic tech today. I'm sure Chief Ferris and Dr. Osborne can help you with those decisions." He glanced over at Lew who nodded in agreement.

"Dr. Osborne?" asked Molly. "Would you mind if I stopped by to talk to you later? You were the last person to see my dad alive and—"

"I would like that, Molly," said Osborne. "I'll give you my address. In fact, why don't you come to my place for dinner this evening?"

"My sister is getting in later this afternoon. Would it be all right if she came along?"

"I'd like to be included," said Lew. "Doc and I fish together and I met your father several times. If you don't mind, I may ask you and your sister some questions regarding your family history and recent conversations you and your father may have had."

"Anything we can do to help you figure this out," said Molly. She stepped closer to Osborne and leaned up to whisper, "Please don't include my stepmother."

"That'll be fine," said Osborne louder than necessary and hoping Patti, still leaning against the barn but watching everyone, hadn't heard Molly's request.

———

Ray kept his boat at a low throttle as he made pretend to search for the right spot to anchor off the submerged sandbar in the middle of the lake, the "honey hole" for walleye that had served him and his clients well until "those three goombahs from Milwaukee" had closed in on him.

He had gotten on the water shortly after three that afternoon, having completed shooting everything around the Pelletier property, both barn and outdoors, that Lew and Bruce had wanted. An official photographer from the Wausau Crime Lab had since taken over the photography to work with Bruce while he directed the on-site investigations of the house and Chuck's office.

Ray wasn't unhappy to see the pesky fishermen. He had a plan: they would see him leave after an hour, return to his dock, and tie up his boat. What they wouldn't see was Ray grab his tackle box and muskie rod, throw them in the back of his pickup, and drive up to the boat landing over on Silver Bass Lake.

Late the night before, he had arranged to borrow a boat from his buddy, Emil Hjelt, and from there he would find his way to Osborne's secret pool on the Loon River. He couldn't wait. It took all the patience he could muster to stay anchored for a full hour, but if he didn't, the three idiots wouldn't believe he was giving up for the day.

Once at the Silver Bass landing, he climbed into Emil's fishing boat, started the outboard, and headed up across the lake and through the channel under the county highway. The river was calm and the boat sped along with a low murmur. Ray scanned the shoreline for the eagles' nest, found it, and cut the motor. He would row the rest of the way so he could study the weed beds below, look for sunken logs that might damage a propeller, and mentally prepare for a fine afternoon of fishing.

When he felt lined up, he dropped anchor, stood up, and cast. The bucktail sailed high and landed in with a soft "plop." Just above the spot where the lure had landed, Ray saw movement. A man was squatting on all fours on a rock not fifty yards away.

"Great—another goddamn nosy son-of-a-bitch," said Ray under his breath. He couldn't believe his bad luck.

The man onshore waved and shouted across the water, "Can I ask you something?"

Ray retrieved his lure, set down the muskie rod, and dipping the oars into the water, he made his way slowly, diagonally toward the shoreline, taking care not to cross the pool into which he had hoped to cast. As he neared the figure on the rock, he could see the man was dressed in khaki shorts and a T-shirt. He had fair skin and hair and when he stood he appeared to be about Ray's height but likely older.

"Thank you," said the man, walking toward Ray, who was

still sitting in the boat. "I want to know what you are fishing for if you don't mind." He stuck his hand out. "Peter Bailey from New Zealand. Thinking about fishing here but not sure what I'm after. We got salmon and trout down under."

"Oh yeah," said Ray, relieved at the sound of the stranger's accent. "Whereabouts in New Zealand?" he asked as he climbed out of the boat and reached to shake the newcomer's hand. He was open to chatting now that he could tell the man was only after simple information. In fact, maybe—if he handled this well—he might even have a new client.

"North Island. Are you familiar with New Zealand?"

"Not really," said Ray, "hear about it on the news once in a while. You have earthquakes, don't you?" Before the man could answer, Ray decided to pitch his services. "I'm fishing for muskie, which is a trophy fish in these parts. Hard to catch. The females are the big ones and we call 'em 'the fish of ten thousand casts.'

"Not to sound immodest, by the way"—he introduced his signature pause—"but . . . I'm a local . . . expert. For example, this afternoon, if . . . all goes well and the wind is to my back and . . . the good Lord overhead . . . I might land a forty-incher weighing over twenty pounds." He waited for the look of astonishment sure to cross Peter Bailey's face.

"I get brown trout weighing twenty-two pounds."

"No. Trout? That big?" Ray was the one astonished.

"Yes, and I understand the trout around here are much smaller. . . ."

"I got people you need to meet," said Ray. "No kidding. *A twenty-two-pound trout?* Then why the hell are you fishing in the northwoods of Wisconsin for God's sake?"

"Working up here for the Northern Forest Resorts operation. I'm designing their fly-fishing preserve."

"You mean the Partridge Lodge development?"

"Right. We have some extraordinary hunting and fishing lodges like the Huka Lodge outside Taupo on the North Island. That's my field—designing preserves like that. When I leave here, there's a new place in Montana I'll be working on. I'll be in the States another nine months or so."

"Did you know the fella that was killed yesterday?" asked Ray.

"What are you talking about? I haven't heard a thing. I took yesterday and today off to get in some hiking, which is how I found my way here. Have had my phone off, too. So, tell me, who was killed? And how? An accident?"

"The CFO for the company you're working for—Chuck Pelletier. He was found dead late yesterday morning. The medical examiner has pretty much said it was foul play. Do you know the guy?"

Peter gave Ray a long, searching look. "How do you know this?"

Ray raised a hand, as if to excuse what he was about to say. "It's a long story but I'm often deputized to help with investigations. I'm not a bad photographer so the Loon Lake Police will have me shoot a crime scene since the nearest crime lab is an hour away in Wausau and, since we have a woman chief of police, the crime lab director likes to drag his feet responding to her requests."

Ray grinned. "I help her get around that razzbonya by not letting so much time go by that trace evidence gets compromised. Chief Ferris appreciates my efforts enough that she doesn't bug me if I have a joint or two."

Peter did not return Ray's grin. Instead his eyes had darkened. "So you were there this morning?"

"Yes."

"Ray," Peter spoke deliberately, "this man who was killed is someone with whom I have been working closely. We were scheduled to meet tomorrow and I'm hoping he wasn't killed because . . ." He paused. "I should meet with your authorities."

Ray shrugged. "I hear you, man. Much as I was planning to cast a bucktail or two, I think you better come with me. Got a car nearby?"

"No. I hiked down here from where I'm staying, next-door to the offices where Chuck was working."

"Got a backpack or anything? You're coming with me in the boat after I make this call."

Lew answered her personal cell phone, spoke with Ray, and then turned to Bruce. "Looks like you better follow me to Doc's place. Ray just met up with someone who may know something related to Pelletier's death."

CHAPTER FOURTEEN

Osborne sat down in the IT office assigned to Dani to watch her scroll through the e-mails in Chuck's laptop computer. "Tell me if you see one you want me to pause so you can read it," said Dani.

"I will," said Osborne. "Chief Ferris asked me to review these with you in case I recognize something but I don't know his business per se so the only ones I'm likely to flag are any from his colleague, Maxwell Gordon, or from his family like his wife and daughters. You tell me if you see some we should examine more carefully."

"Here's what I think, Dr. Osborne," said Dani, her fingers dancing over the computer keys as speedily as if she were one of Osborne's grandchildren texting on a cell phone, "since neither of us know what we're looking for exactly, let's get familiar with all the e-mails that he's received over the last week.

"As Chief Ferris and Bruce or any of the techs from the crime lab learn more and tell us more, then we can go back through with a better idea of what we're looking for. Make sense?"

"Does for me," said Osborne. "Keep in mind you're dealing

with an old man who is so technologically challenged he can barely change channels on his new smart TV—so you take the lead."

Dani laughed and continued to scroll.

———————

Dani Wright had been a cosmetology student at the local tech college when Lew discovered that while she showed promise as a hairdresser, when it came to computers she was, as her beginning computer science instructor put it: "outstanding." Even better with smartphones on which she could text like a madman.

After commandeering the young woman, who wore her hair in an explosion of brunette curls cascading over her shoulders, to help with an investigation requiring sophisticated database research, Lew had offered her a part-time position as the IT "guru" for the Loon Lake Police Department until she could earn her degree in computer science.

Dani wasn't convinced it was wise to trade the security of the hair salon ("women *always* need highlights," her boss had argued) for "the cops" until Lew convinced the Loon Lake City Council to make her a salary offer Lew was convinced she couldn't refuse. When Dani hesitated to accept the offer, Lew had badgered her saying, "Dani, unless I have a felony crime investigation you will always have holidays and weekends off so you can still do hair. . . ."

That, plus the promise of health benefits, was all it took. "*All?*" Lew exclaimed, with a laugh and raised eyebrows, when describing the negotiations to Osborne later. "By the time she said 'yes,' I was exhausted."

At the moment, it was not looking like there would be many ladies getting highlights, weaves, or foils over the next few days: Dani's magic fingers on the computer keyboard were going to be in high demand. She had just brought up Chuck's e-mails from that morning when she and Osborne heard a commotion in the hallway.

It was Ray barging into Lew's office with Peter Bailey in tow. Lew and Bruce Peters were sitting at the table and chairs fronting the windows facing south where they had been studying the reports from Bruce and his colleagues who had finished scouring the barn and the Pelletier home for trace evidence.

"Sorry to interrupt, Chief," said Ray, talking so fast Lew found it alarming. "But since you insisted you didn't have time to meet us at Doc's right away, I am making an executive decision: you have to meet this man. Now."

Too surprised to answer, Lew waved Ray and his friend into the room. "Okay, okay. The floor is all yours, Ray."

"All righty, then," said Ray, happy to take the stage and extending an arm to indicate Peter. "I ran into this guy up on the Loon River. He's been working closely with Chuck Pelletier on that whole fishing preserve—"

"The Partridge Lodge project?" asked Lew.

"Yes, I'm the consultant on the project—Peter Bailey," said Peter as he stepped forward to extend a hand to Lew and to Bruce as they introduced themselves.

"I can tell from your accent you're not from Wisconsin," said Bruce. "Australia?"

"New Zealand. The guys running Northern Forest Resorts

out of New York hired me to design and build a trout fishery like the ones we have on the North and South Islands. Maybe you've heard of the Huka Lodge? It's world famous.

"I used to be a fly-fishing coordinator there. So when I was telling Ray here that I've had some questions on the construction I've been hired to oversee and that I was supposed to be meeting with Chuck tomorrow—"

"'Questions' isn't the right word," said Ray, interrupting. "Tell them, Peter—you've seeing some . . . e . . . reg . . . u . . . larities, shall we say?"

"Ray, you mean 'irregularities'?" asked Lew, sounding testy. This wasn't the moment to fool around.

"Yep. Sorry," said Ray sheepishly.

"Sit down, Mr. Bailey," said Lew, pointing to a chair across the table from her. "You, too, Ray—got a new assignment for you by the way. After we hear from Mr. Bailey."

"Peter," corrected the newcomer, "call me Peter, please." Taking the chair across from Lew he sat while saying, "Let me start by telling you what I've been responsible for. I'll try to keep it short. Okay?"

"Take all the time you want," said Lew.

"Do you mind if I tape what you're about to tell us?" asked Bruce.

"Not if you think it's necessary."

Peter waited for Bruce to get his tape recorder ready. "I have one in my smartphone but this is more reliable," said Bruce, apologizing as he reached to pull out a tape recorder and stand from a backpack. "Ready."

"For the record, my name is Peter Bailey," said Peter with a half-smile, "and I live in Taupo on the North Island of New

Zealand. I am trained as a fishery biologist and I am a principal with River and Stream Consulting. Our main office is in Auckland but I work all over both islands.

"I was hired ten months ago by Northern Forests Resorts to build a thirty-mile trout fishery here in northern Wisconsin. For this project, I have designed man-made streams featuring shoals and wide, shallow stretches of riffles—ideal for trout.

"Also, on the existing waterways, I've been directing stream reparation efforts, including planting undercut banks with wetland grasses designed to protect trout from eagles and to attract good insect hatches. And we're in the midst of restoring a natural spring creek. I guess you would call me 'the project manager.'

"Where this gets interesting for you people is that I have been overseeing the purchase and installation of computer-controlled pumps that will regulate the temperature and flow rate in the streams; and the construction of three bridges. I've also directed the purchase of a number of old barns and homesteads that were in the way of our streambed development. Some are so dilapidated they're in danger of collapsing into the waterways."

He paused. "Tell them the problem," said Ray, shifting in his chair.

"Wait," said Lew, "before you say more. One of my deputies, Dr. Paul Osborne, is working down the hall. I want him to hear this, too." She called down to Dani's office.

Osborne joined the group around the table and after introductions Lew gave him a brief update on what Peter had said so far.

"So here's the issue I have and that I was planning to discuss with Chuck Pelletier tomorrow," said Peter. "I submit invoices monthly for my time as well as invoices I receive from the contractors who are instructed to report to me first.

"This past Monday—for no reason other than I had time on my hands and was looking to update my project management report—I asked to review the previous month's invoices. When I looked them over, I discovered someone had inflated the totals on the costs of the pumps and the construction materials for the bridges. These were not the invoices I had submitted and I was able to double-check against what I have in my laptop, which I keep with me at all times.

"Not only that—my initials, which indicate I'm approving the invoice—were forged.

"Furthermore, it looked to me like the payments were going to an entity I'm not familiar with: different contractor, different company from the one that had been receiving payments.

"Worse yet from my perspective, the inflated invoices make it look like I'm building *sixty* miles of trout stream—not thirty. And a bridge that never ends. The changes are outrageous if not illegal, and that's what I wanted to discuss with Chuck."

"How many people know about this?" asked Lew. "Know what you've discovered, that is?"

"Only Chuck—and the individual who altered those invoices."

"And who sees those invoices besides Chuck?"

"Well, the contractors submitting the originals, of course. Then, as CEO on the entire development, Gordon Maxwell should review them, but as far as I know he doesn't do anything with the financials or the invoices. At least, that's what Chuck said. My understanding has been that as CFO, Chuck's the one who keeps track of the finances and he is the person who, after my approvals, submits them for payment."

"I see," said Lew, thinking. "Since you wanted to talk to Chuck, it sounds like you trusted him. Correct?"

"Yes. I will be very surprised if—"

"Who do you think is behind this?"

"Might be the bridge guy. Tom Patterson. He worries me. Nothing I can put my finger on, but his invoices on the one bridge and the pumps, which we've been buying through him, are the ones altered."

"Has this happened just once? This past month?"

"I'm not sure. I haven't had time to check back a few months. I was going to check with Chuck before doing that."

"And only you and Chuck Pelletier have access to the invoices?"

"Now that is a good question," said Peter. "Not necessarily. Because of the sketchy Internet reception in this region, we've asked that all the contractors submit their invoices on hard copy.

"They are to drop them into Chuck's in-box, which is on his secretary's desk, by late Thursday every week. I go through those, enter the costs into an Excel chart, which I print out and place in a manila folder along with the invoices. That folder goes into Chuck's in-box—from me—late Friday afternoon. My understanding is that he picks it up first thing Monday morning."

"But it stays on the secretary's desk over the weekend?" asked Bruce. "Sounds like there's a fair amount of traffic through that office?"

"Plenty of traffic. Guys stop in for coffee and doughnuts in the morning, some fellas meet me there when they have questions on something. Lots of people coming and going." He nodded. "It's a busy place."

"Doc," said Lew, turning to Osborne, "let's see if Dani can get into the financial records, too. Peter, you will have earlier copies of your Excel reports so you can check and see if the alterations have happened before?"

"Yes, and I have checked off and on, but this is the first time the money involved was significant. There was enough of an increase in costs to boost my original estimate from fifteen to twenty million dollars."

"I see," said Lew. "Peter, where are you staying?"

"I rent a small cottage down the road from the Partridge Lodge development offices."

"I'd like your address and phone number," said Lew. "I'm going to give you my personal cell number, too, in case anything else occurs to you. And, Peter, keep an eye out."

"Me?" He sounded surprised.

"You. If you see anything out of the ordinary around your place, let me know and I'll have the Loon Lake Police or Oneida County sheriff put your cottage under surveillance."

"But—"

"Peter," said Lew, "all we know right now is that Chuck Pelletier was murdered. By whom or why we have no idea . . . yet. It could be related to the financial shenanigans you just outlined for us or it could be a random killing by someone on drugs looking for money. But I do not want to take chances and certainly don't want another victim."

"You really think someone would . . . ?"

"I don't know what to think until we know more. In the meantime, keep a sharp eye."

Lew was getting to her feet when they heard a light knock on the door, which stood open. Dani poked her head in and said, "Chief Ferris? Doc, Bruce—I think you should see this one e-mail. It's the last one Mr. Pelletier sent before he left his office yesterday. I didn't think it was anything until a few minutes ago. He had sent a question to someone and they just got back to him. You need to see this. . . ."

As everyone except Ray and Peter started to follow Dani back to her office, Ray said, "Wait! Before you do that, I want Peter to tell you about the twenty-two-pound brown trout he caught down in New Zealand. . . ."

"Really?" asked Lew. "I don't have time to hear about it now."

"Tell you what, Ray," said Doc. "We're busy tonight. I've asked Chuck's daughters to come by my place tonight for dinner. Lew and I are going to help them with the arrangements for their father. Why don't you and Peter join the two of us for breakfast tomorrow morning? We can talk about that trout then."

Ray threw a glance at Peter before saying, "Sure. But how 'bout early, early? I've promised our buddy here to show him some big girls—bigger'n those trout of his."

"Six a.m. sound good?" asked Lew. "That works for me. . . ."

"Fine," said Ray. "My place. I'm cooking."

"Can I join you?" asked Bruce, a hopeful look on his face. "Anything trout works for me. I'll bring doughnuts."

"Dani, you're the only person left out," said Osborne. "Would you like to come for breakfast, too?"

Dani laughed. "Thank you but no. That is way too early for this girl."

CHAPTER FIFTEEN

Peter, thank you for taking the time to come in today," said Lew as Ray and Peter stood at the door, ready to leave her office. She looked over at Ray. "Now don't forget before you truck off fishing again, I have another job for you."

"That's what you said and, hey, every penny counts," said Ray with a goofy grin. "Can you tell me what it is now? Or do you want to give me a call later?"

Osborne could tell he was quite pleased having stumbled onto Peter Bailey. Probably took it as a sign of his brilliance rather than just plain dumb luck. Osborne reminded himself not to be critical of the man who had braved a blizzard to get the late Mary Lee to the emergency room in spite of knowing she continually badgered the Loon Lake county clerk in hopes of getting Ray's trailer home condemned.

"Now is fine," said Lew. "This will take two seconds. Earlier today Chuck's daughter, Molly, told us that a piece of driftwood that had been hanging on the wall in the room where we found Chuck's body is missing. She noticed it right away and said that was odd as it's sort of a family heirloom and her dad would never have discarded it. She described the driftwood as being shaped like a cane but it sounded more like a club to me."

"So you want me to walk the property? See if I can find it?"

"I would start around the barn," said Lew. "The sooner the better."

"Sure, I'll get started right now," said Ray. "What color is the driftwood? Dark? Light? Mottled?"

"Bleached almost white. She and her dad found it on a beach when they were sailing in Chesapeake Bay back when she was a kid." She glanced over at Peter, who was listening. "Your buddy Ray here's got the eyes of an eagle," said Lew. "I count on him to find the impossible."

A quizzical expression crossed Peter's face. "Not sure what that means," he said, "we don't have eagles in New Zealand."

"Owls?" asked Lew.

"Oh, yes, the Morepork owl is one of our predators. Hunts at night just like your owls, and it has a haunting, melancholy call."

"Ray," said Lew, "do one of your loon calls for Peter."

Ray obliged, causing a few heads to turn down at the end of the hall where Marlaine on Dispatch and the receptionist were sitting. When Ray had finished, Peter applauded.

"Ah, maybe you are part 'ruru,' " he said with a grin, "that's the Maori name for the Morepork owl."

"Later, you two," said Lew with a wave as she and Osborne hurried to follow Dani back to her office.

———————

Sitting alongside Dani, Lew and Osborne took a few minutes to read the e-mail that Chuck Pelletier had sent to the executive with the Florida condominium development. After identifying himself as the CFO with the Northern Forest Resorts, Chuck had written that they were hoping to involve Gordon Maxwell in some new strategic planning efforts and asked for any suggestions that the executive, as a former colleague of Maxwell's, might have as to how they could maximize working with Maxwell.

"A politic way of asking if they had any problems with the guy," said Osborne after reading the e-mail twice.

"I agree," said Lew.

"Well, here is that man's response to the question," said Dani before sitting back to let Osborne and Lew digest what they were about to see.

> Gordon Maxwell? We fired that guy years ago. And we aren't the only ones who had problems with that individual. I am not going to go on the record and say more because I don't need a lawsuit. Give me a call and I'll tell you who to talk to.

At the bottom of the e-mail was the man's name and title, the name of the firm he worked for, and the firm's website and contact information, including a direct number for reaching the writer of the e-mail himself.

Osborne, who had been reading over Lew's shoulder, was not surprised when she picked up her cell phone and punched in the man's direct number. "I'll put him on speaker," said Lew while they listened to the phone ringing.

A low, gravelly voice answered.

After identifying herself, Lew said, "I'm calling because Mr. Chuck Pelletier with the Northern Forest Resorts, who sent you an e-mail yesterday morning, is no longer alive. He died hours after sending that e-mail. We're not yet sure of the circumstances but I'm with law enforcement and I just read your response. Do you have a few minutes for questions?"

"Yes and no," said the man. "For legal reasons, I prefer not to say much other than I consider the man, Gordon Maxwell, a pathological liar, and I am happy to point out that he did not last long with our company. The person you need to talk to is Hugh Aronson. He's a reporter with our local business journal and he wrote a very effective exposé that basically ran your guy out of town. Let me give you his phone number. Sorry I can't say more, but good luck."

"Thank you," said Lew, writing down the phone number he offered. She clicked off her cell phone and looked around at Osborne and Dani. "Are we ready?" she asked.

"Do you want to record the call?" asked Dani.

"I need his permission to do that," said Lew, "so let's see what he says first." She placed a call to the number she was just given and a younger-sounding male voice answered.

"Hello, this is Hugh Aronson."

Again Lew identified herself and gave a brief description of the reason for her call. She did not mention Chuck Pelletier's death but only that she was interested in background information on a Gordon Maxwell: "He's running a large company up here and several residents have complained about some recent real estate negotiations. . . ."

She cited Lorraine's allegation that she had been persuaded to sell for too low a price. When she had finished, the man on the other end chuckled. "So our boy is up to shenanigans way up north?"

"Maybe," said Lew, "but we don't know much about him

other than that he is the CEO of this multi-million-dollar resort development up here. I'd like to know what you know."

"Sure. I'll e-mail up half a dozen stories I did on the guy three years ago. Let me point out, however, that he is slippery. The guy has never been indicted, but he is a career criminal. You'll like my stories. They lay it all out, and I don't mind mentioning that I won awards for several of them. My only regret is that Maxwell left this town and disappeared before anyone could indict him."

"Do you mind telling me a little more? And is it all right for me to tape this conversation?"

"Go right ahead," said Hugh. "What Maxwell did was capitalize on all the condo development happening down here. He specialized in kickback schemes targeted at small companies desperate to make a buck. And old people—he was great at charming elderly ladies into loaning him cash from their 401Ks with the promise he would invest it for them. Which, of course, he didn't.

"By the time people caught on to what he was up to, he was long gone and any witnesses to his crooked deals had been paid off. Oh, be aware he is quite the ladies' man, too. He always has one on his arm and she's suckered in to provide alibis when he needs 'em. Quite the operator.

"Of course, what the ladies never know is he has a wife and three kids in Kentucky. Or *had*—she divorced him after my stories ran.

"But, like I say, he slipped away from the authorities down here real easy. Given what you've told me, you'll appreciate my articles."

"I have one last question," said Lew, "how does he get

hired by people like the hedge fund that owns the development company up here?"

"Oh, hey," said Aronson with a note of derision, "they're smart guys. They went to Harvard Business School. They have confidence in *their* assessment of his résumé, his lies. You think they'd run a background check? Hell, no, they know what they're doing . . . until it's too late." He chuckled again.

"Look, I'm late for an editorial meeting. Be about an hour or two before I can check my backup hard drive for those stories. May take me until tomorrow morning but I'll get 'em to you. Does that work?"

"I can't thank you enough," said Lew and gave him e-mail addresses for herself and Dani. She set the phone down and said, "Wow. I'm stunned. I think it goes without saying that we're on to something."

"Wow," echoed Osborne and Dani together.

CHAPTER SIXTEEN

Osborne walked through his living room, rearranging for the fifth time the two bowls he'd set out holding a mix of nuts, raisins, and cranberries. Lew strolled out of his bedroom, where she had changed from her uniform into tan slacks and a soft cream-colored long-sleeved pullover, and paused to watch.

"Nervous, Doc?"

"Not sure if I'm nervous, worried, or just getting old," said Osborne with a slight smile. "What do you say to two young women who just lost the most important person in their world? 'Sorry' is hardly adequate."

"Given what you've told me about their dad, I have a hunch they're pretty strong individuals and handling this better than you might expect. I would say just give them room to do or say whatever feels right to them."

As a knock sounded at the door off the mudroom, Osborne hurried past the kitchen to open it. "Is this the right door?" asked Molly. "Should we be going around to the front of the house?"

"Heck, no," said Osborne. "No one ever uses the front door. Come right in." He stepped back as Molly walked in, followed by a slender, shorter girl, whose long wavy hair was so blond it was almost white.

"And you must be Jessie." Osborne put out his hand. Beckoning toward Lew, who was standing behind him, he said, "Molly, you met Chief Ferris earlier today. Jessie, this is Loon Lake's chief of police, Lewellyn Ferris. She is also one of my close friends."

"And she's working on Dad's case," said Molly, turning to her sister. "Dr. Osborne is helping with the investigation, too."

"We can talk about that later," said Lew as she shook each girl's hand. "More important is to hear how the two of you are managing. This has got to be difficult."

"Lew's right," said Osborne. "Let's all head for the living room." He pointed the way. "Dinner is pretty basic tonight, I'm afraid—pizza. But it's our favorite from the Birchwood Bar, which is halfway between here and Rhinelander."

"Works for me—I haven't eaten all day," said Molly with a grateful smile.

The girls walked past him to follow Lew into the living room, and Osborne noticed again that they were as different in appearance as his own daughters. If he'd met them under different circumstances, he never would have guessed them to be sisters. Molly, dark-haired, strong-boned, and stalwart, was not unlike his daughter Mallory, while Jessie, so slim and fair, reminded him of Erin.

He was struck by how composed the two sisters seemed. At least that was true of Molly, though her eyes were ever so slightly red-rimmed. So he was surprised when he saw Lew stop, put an arm around Jessie, and ask the younger woman,

"Are you okay? You're shaking. Here, sit down and take it easy. You've been through a lot over the last twenty-four hours. We understand."

"No, that isn't it," said Molly, hovering over her sister. "She just had a really bad scare at the airport."

"*What*?" Lew and Osborne asked in unison.

"Yeah," said Molly. "I told Jessie to meet me over in the hangar where I was checking on my plane and some guy walked up and grabbed her. Grabbed her and kissed her."

"Wait, wait—start over, please," said Osborne. "Say that again? A *stranger* grabbed you, Jessie?"

"Yes, please," said Lew, echoing his concern. "What hangar, what plane, and who—?"

"Didn't Dad tell you I'm a pilot?" asked Molly. "I fly for Delta. And I have my own plane—a Piper Comanche. That's how I got here."

As she spoke, Osborne remembered now how Chuck had bragged about Molly's career in a field traditionally male. He had pointed out that she had followed in the footsteps of her maternal grandfather, an aeronautics engineer, who taught her to fly when she was only ten years old.

"She and that old man were inseparable," Chuck had said with pride. "Jessie, on the other hand, is the opposite of her sister—quiet, artistic. She's a graphic designer like her mom. And she's happy, too. They're both doing what's right for them." Chuck had been so proud of both girls.

"So Jessie knew I would be over in that hangar where private planes are kept," Molly was saying. "She was on her way in to catch up with me when this guy walks by her, stops, turns around. . . . Jess, you tell them."

The young woman's hands were visibly shaking as she spoke. "This guy walked by me and he, um, he turned around, I guess, and walked back in the other direction to grab me and, um, kiss me. Like, hard. Right on the mouth. Then he walked off without saying anything—just grabbed me, and . . . I mean, he didn't really *hurt* me. It was so fast, so weird. I've never had that happen before." She looked ready to cry.

Sitting down beside Jessie, Lew put an arm around her shoulder and said, "Tell me what this person looked like."

"You know, all I can say is he was wearing a business suit, he's not very tall and he's got this weird hair—like wiry and stiff. But it all happened so fast, I didn't get a good look at his face. I, um, blanked it out, I think."

"And this happened in the hangar, not over in the terminal?" asked Lew.

"Yeah, in the hangar. Down the back hall by the restrooms. I had just come out of the ladies' room." Jessie calmed down as she spoke.

"Let me get you something to drink," said Osborne. "A beer, glass of wine, a soda?"

"Just water, please," said Jessie, with a nervous toss of her long hair. "I'm still kind of upset." She gave a weak laugh.

"You girls will be here for a few days, won't you?" asked Lew. "I'll pull together some photos of men who have been arrested for crimes against women. We'll see if you can identify the individual who accosted you." Jessie looked uncertain.

"He didn't really do anything *bad*." She spoke hesitantly.

"I'll decide that," said Lew. "Grabbing someone and kissing them without their consent is not allowed. But enough of this right now. On a better note, I thought you'd like to know that your father's body was released from the Wausau Crime Lab morgue late this afternoon. You are free to make your funeral arrangements."

"Yes, I had a call from the funeral home," said Molly. "Jessie and I plan to have a brief service the day after tomorrow. Just his secretary, that man he worked for, maybe you folks? After that, he'll be cremated and we'll take his ashes back east to bury near our mom."

Aware that she hadn't mentioned Patti, Osborne said, "And you're including your stepmother, of course. . . ."

"She doesn't want to come. She thinks Jessie and I are crazy that we want a memorial service and an open casket."

"It's a tradition in our family," said Jessie, chiming in. "For Molly and me, it's our way of finding some closure. We had an open casket for our mom and our grandparents. See, whatever or however our dad died, the important thing for us is to see him at peace. For people who knew him to see him that way. We really, really want that."

"But Patti doesn't. She told me she can't bear it," said Molly. "But what the hell? She knew our dad for all of two and a half years. We've known him all our lives. Our decision, don't you think?"

Molly caught Jessie's eye. "There's another reason we're

keeping her out of this. I know it sounds awful, but we're not . . . close. My dad shared some things with me in the last month or so that made me so angry with that woman that the less I have to deal with her, the better.

"Do you know that without asking my dad, she sold all our mother's jewelry? Took it out of his bureau drawer without asking and sold it!"

"It wasn't hers to sell," said Jessie in a soft voice. "It was ours. Dad didn't even know it was gone until he looked for it a couple months ago. He was planning to give me this wonderful necklace for my birthday. He and Mom bought it in China years ago. She loved it. Wore it all the time." A tear slipped down Jessie's cheek.

"Plus she was always gone from the house whenever he would go home for lunch," said Molly, her voice rising. "He told me she doesn't have any women friends so he wondered where she was, but she insisted she was working out. Like *four hours* working out? Give me a break. Dad didn't say as much but I think he thought she might be fooling around."

"He told me he knew she was pretty disappointed when they moved here and he didn't want to socialize," said Jessie. "Patti loves parties. She loves to cook for people—"

"Are you kidding? Don't tell me you're apologizing for her," said Molly, turning on her sister.

With a shrug Jessie wilted. "Not really, just saying, you know?"

The fury in Molly's eyes sparked a change of mind for Osborne. Earlier he had decided not to mention Chuck's early-morning phone call and his accusation. But listening to

Molly's and Jessie's stories about Patti changed his thinking. It must have done the same for Lew because she caught the look in his eye and gave a slight nod of agreement.

"Not trying to change the subject, Molly and Jessie," said Lew, "but what, if anything, did your father tell you about a man he has been working with—Gordon Maxwell?"

Both girls shook their heads. "Not much," said Molly, "only that when it came to the finance stuff he thought the guy was in over his head. Like he didn't really know what he was doing. That's all. But our father never really talked business with us."

"I was hesitant to share this earlier," said Osborne, "but Chief Ferris and I think it would be wise for you to be aware of some . . . disturbing information." Again Osborne saw approval in Lew's eyes. He plunged ahead.

"Very early the day your father was killed, he came here to my house and told me that earlier that morning as he walked up the driveway after getting his mail, Gordon Maxwell came at him in his SUV and tried to run him over."

The girls stared at Osborne.

"Chuck felt sure it was deliberate."

Molly glanced off to one side. "I don't know . . . there's that one curve where you absolutely cannot see who's coming. . . ."

"Did anyone else see it happen?" It was Jessie who asked the question.

This time Lew signaled for Osborne to say no more. Too late—Molly had seen Lew catch his eye.

"Why do you ask?" said Lew.

Jessie shrugged. "I just . . . well . . . Okay, Molly didn't go to the wedding when Dad married Patti. Just me—"

"They decided last minute and I was scheduled to fly that week," said Molly, "or I would have."

"But I did go," said Jessie. "And during this little reception they had, two women who knew Patti took me aside to tell me to keep an eye on her. They said she was very 'clingy' around men. They said they'd always made sure to keep her away from their husbands because she was so . . . clingy. It sounded to me like they thought she was after their husbands so they were happy she was married and moving away.

"So ever since my dad has been sounding so unhappy on our phone calls these last couple months I've been thinking that something was wrong at home, you know?"

"Jessie was my dad's favorite," said Molly. "He always told her more than he ever told me."

"So, I am wondering, you know?" Jessie gave a shrug of her shoulders as she spoke.

"You should tell them, Doc," said Lew. "I've heard enough that I think it's important the girls know what we know."

"Your father told me he saw Patti in the car with Maxwell. That's what he said. Now that is all we know. I wanted him to drive into Loon Lake right then to tell Chief Ferris what had happened but he insisted on going to his office first . . . for a conference call."

Osborne put his head down, pressed the fingers of his right hand against his eyelids, and took a deep breath. "For a goddamn conference call . . . he never came back."

A hand patted his shoulder. He glanced up into Molly's face. "It's all right, Dr. Osborne. Please, it's not your fault. Dad always did things his way."

"Yeah," said Jessie, "like marrying that bimbo."

"Look," said Molly—it was her turn to put an arm around Jessie—"he was so lonely after Mom died. Patti was *there*. She cooked great meals for him. I think, I mean, I know he didn't realize the kind of friendship he and Mom had in their marriage was unique. You know?" She looked around at Lew and Osborne. "It's not easy to find that in a person. Friendship, I mean."

"Tell me," said Osborne, thinking of his thirty years with a woman whose face fell whenever he opened his mouth to speak.

———————

But now at least, even though I have so few years of life left, mused Osborne to himself, as he often did these days, now I am well aware how fortunate I am to have stumbled onto Lewellyn Ferris even if it was in a trout stream. He would grin to himself at the memory. Yep, Lew is a treasure—her warmth, her willingness to share, and the ongoing mystery of who she is. The sheer fun of knowing her even if she does catch more fish than I do.

———————

"We weren't going to mention what your father told Dr. Osborne that morning," said Lew, "but it has significant bearing on my investigation. I've shared it with Bruce Peters, one of the Wausau boys whom Molly met earlier today."

"'Wausau boys'?" asked Jessie.

"The forensic experts from the Wausau Crime Lab," said Lew. "I call them 'the Wausau boys' for short."

"Dr. Osborne, Chief Ferris," said Molly, "now that I know

you're interested in that Maxwell guy, there's something else you should be aware of. When I was at the airport checking on my plane, I walked by one in the same hangar that really needs some repairs. I mentioned it to the guy there who gives flying lessons and he agreed.

"He said it's a shame how the owner doesn't take care of it. He lies about the inspections and is sloppy when it comes to required maintenance. He said the plane, a Beechcraft Bonanza, is an accident waiting to happen—and guess who owns it? Gordon Maxwell."

"That must mean he's back in Loon Lake," said Lew. "How interesting. He was supposed to call the station the minute he returned. I'll check with Bruce. Maybe he's heard something."

CHAPTER SEVENTEEN

Osborne and Lew woke to a sunbeam streaming through the open bedroom window. It was only 5:00 a.m. but the sunlight bouncing off the top of the bureau was so promising Osborne couldn't help feeling better than he had in the last two days.

"Coffee, dear?" Climbing back under the light summer quilt, he grinned as he handed a warm mug of black coffee to his bedmate. Lew pushed herself up against the pillows and with a grateful smile reached for the cup.

"Did he really say *a twenty-two-pound* brown trout?" she asked Osborne as he climbed into the bed beside her. "That is impossible."

"Likely one of Ray's usual bad jokes. Pardon me—one of Ray's *embellishments* is more accurate. What do you want to bet the truth is closer to *two* pounds? We'll know shortly. We're due at Ray's for breakfast at six. With Peter and Bruce there, he'll have to tone it down."

"You think," said Lew with a snort. "Has Ray Pradt ever toned it down?" The two of them sipped happily as they listened to the busy chatter of Osborne's winged neighbors.

———

"So tell us the truth, Peter," said Lew as she sat down to Ray's breakfast table with a full plate of eggs scrambled with sharp cheddar cheese, two lightly sautéed bluegill fillets, and a slice of homemade bread, "does New Zealand really have twenty-two-pound brown trout or did Ray make that up?"

"Let me ask *you* something," said Peter Bailey as he slathered butter on his toast. "Do you really have fifty-inch muskies?"

"We do. Care for some thimbleberry jam?" Lew pushed the small jar Peter's way.

"Wow," said Peter after a bite of his toast. "Ray, did you make this?"

"You're avoiding the question," said Lew.

"He didn't make it," said Osborne. "He delivers strings of bluegills to a couple elderly ladies here and they keep him stocked with jams and breads and . . ."

"Cranberry muffins," said Ray. Sitting beside Ray, Bruce had his mouth full but kept nodding as everyone spoke, his bushy eyebrows raised high with delight. Osborne couldn't be sure if he was happy with his breakfast or the questions.

"To answer your question now that I'm finished chewing," said Peter, wiping his mouth with a paper napkin. "Yes, we have twenty-two-pound brown trout. Large rainbows, too. But those are trophy fish. A ten-pounder is considered a very nice catch. And, yes, relative to the rest of the world, our trout may not be native but they are massive."

"Same goes for our muskies," said Bruce, anxious to chime in. "Fifty inches is remarkable but any one of us is happy with a thirty-six or forty-incher. My question for you is how does it happen that your trout get so big? A different species than ours, maybe?"

"No," said Peter, "but we have a much more temperate climate and I would have to say that with a total population of four million people on both islands, New Zealand waters are lightly fished in contrast to yours. With only a few exceptions, too, I have to brag that our rivers and streams, thanks to the glaciers, are so pristine you can drink from them.

"We have so much water. Where I live, which is near Lake Taupo on the North Island, I have twenty-five rivers within an hour. Another town not that far away, Rotorua, has eleven rivers and fifteen lakes nearby."

"Loon Lake has three hundred and fifty lakes within a five-mile radius of here," said Lew. "Over a thousand lakes in our county."

"Hey, you're in *my* wheelhouse," said Bruce. "This whole lake region of northern Wisconsin has the highest ratio of water to land in the world—more than Minnesota, more than anywhere in Russia." Everyone stared at him as he set his fork down on his empty plate and looked around the table with an air of satisfaction. "And that's scientific," he added.

"I certainly won't argue how much water we all have," said Peter. "Afraid the bottom line is we do have bigger trout."

"How do you fish those?" asked Osborne, enjoying another swig of coffee.

"Same as you," said Peter. "Although one difference that I've noticed since I've been working on the Partridge Lodge project is that we wade slower because we are not allowed to have felt on our wading boots—to avoid issues with invasive species. So we have rubber-soled boots, and you can take quite a tumble if you move too fast on those.

"But that isn't a problem because we sight fish. Our waters are so clear with currents running over stretches of pea gravel that you can easily see the fish lurking. And vice versa I should add. Because our trout can see us and see colors, one rule I follow is to use a gray or dull brown fly line. Any line that isn't bright."

"What about your leader and tippet?" asked Lew. "Same as what we use?"

"Close. Most of us fish a nine-foot leader with a little tippet on the end. Other than that, we take our time. Most often, you get one shot at dropping your fly by that fish. I sometimes wait fifteen, twenty minutes between casts. One thing I don't do is false cast, especially since our fish spook so easily. That's another reason I tend to fish rivers where I can cast a good twenty feet or more."

Heads nodded around the breakfast table. "Trout flies," said Bruce, "you use a lot of different ones, really work the hatch?"

"Nah, I'm not a purist that way," said Peter. "I have a couple favorites—on a stream I like a Mrs. Simpson, which trout love. It resembles a cockabully, which is kind of like your tiny sculpin. For fishing in lakes, I'll go deep with a Hamills Killer Red Body—looks like a dragonfly. That's the one I'm going to try here."

"Can I come?" asked Bruce, brows high with anxiety.

"Not unless I go, too," said Lew. "I want to see how you load and shoot line when you're casting twenty-five feet. That's one heck of a long cast."

"Count me in," said Osborne, getting to his feet and carrying his plate to the sink.

"Okay, guys, I'm up for it, too," said Ray, surprising Osborne with a sudden and uncharacteristic interest in fly-fishing.

"But not until Doc and Bruce and I find who killed Chuck Pelletier. Fly-fishing has to wait until then, I'm afraid," said Lew.

"Of course," said Peter. "Please, let me know if there's anything more I can do to help. I brought all my invoices with me. They're in my van."

"I'll take those," said Bruce. "We have a forensic accountant on staff who will check them against Pelletier's financial reports. Dani has been able to find those reports on Chuck's laptop and print them off."

"Thank you for the wonderful breakfast, Ray," said Ray with a petulant look on his face.

"Oh gosh, this was so good. Sorry we forgot to say thank you," said Lew as she walked toward the door. She stopped. "Ray, are you still searching the Pelletier property for that driftwood? You would have told me if you found anything. . . ."

"Nothing yet, Chief," said Ray. "I'm going over the entire area again this morning. You'll get a call if I see anything. If you don't need me later, I was going to take Peter out muskie fishing."

"Okay by me so long as you keep your phone nearby."

"Show him our spot," said Osborne.

"You sure about that, Doc?"

Osborne nodded. For all his goofiness, Ray never lacked respect for a friend's secrets—fishing spots and otherwise.

CHAPTER EIGHTEEN

Peter flinched. "Yikes," he said, "that is so loud." He was sitting in the bow of Ray's boat, comfortable in the padded captain's chair when a large bucktail lure had sailed over his head to land fifty feet away with a pleasant plopping sound.

"What?" asked Ray, who was standing near the stern, "something wrong?"

After hitting the Pelletier property at five that morning for one more fruitless search for the missing piece of driftwood, Ray had swung by Peter's cottage, where he woke the New Zealander up.

Two mugs of hot coffee and three glazed doughnuts (each) later, they were headed out. For the "legendary hunting ground for big girls, according to the gospel of Dr. Paul 'Muskie Hunter' Osborne," Ray had said, assuring Peter he had permission to share the location of the secret bay.

"Course, if you weren't a friend of mine this wouldn't be happening," Ray had said, adding that "after landing a fifty-incher all Doc—or myself—will ever tell a nosy fisherman is 'look for the big rock.' Period."

"But there are rocks everywhere," said Peter.

"Right," Ray had said with a smug smile.

———————

"Nothing wrong," said Peter in answer to Ray's question, "just that how you fish these muskies is so different from how we sight fish trout. When I cast, I try not to make a sound. Not even a whisper if I can help it, whether I'm dropping a Mrs. Simpson or a Hamills Killer Red Body."

"That is not how you fish muskie," said Ray. "Not only can muskies hear but they have a lateral line that senses vibrations and movements in water," said Ray. "These fish are predators waiting to ambush a duckling or a frog, even a small bird. They eat other fish, too, of course, but ambush is their game— so the trick is to *lure* them in.

"That's why I like the bucktail: as I reel it toward me, it vibrates. If you watch close you'll see me pull, then stop for a minute to pick up slack in my line, then pull again, and as the lure nears the boat, I'll do a figure eight, keeping the lure in the water. If I've had any luck, you might see a big mother following that bucktail."

"And then?" asked Peter.

"And then I have to set the hook. Which is not as easy as it sounds," said Ray, reeling, then casting again.

"Okay, I'll give it a try," said Peter, getting to his feet. Raising the borrowed muskie rod, he cast forward, following Ray's instructions.

Half an hour later, no muskies in sight, Ray set down his rod and poured each of them a cup of hot coffee from his thermos. "Could be the girls aren't hungry this morning," he said.

"I'm a night man myself. Guiding I take most of my clients out right around dusk."

"Oh, yeah?" asked Peter as he sent his bucktail out across the water. "Say, what are those drawings I saw on the desk at your place? Look like coffins. Am I wrong?"

"I'm experimenting," said Ray. "When my guiding business is slow, I dig graves for the Catholic cemetery here and I've been thinking of getting into the coffin business. Kind of a guaranteed business opportunity, y'know," he said with a grin.

"Some Amish fellas I know are making a killing—sorry for the pun—with nice wood coffins, so why not me? I haven't sold one yet—just getting started." He sipped from his coffee.

"Lots of people do that in New Zealand, which is why I asked," said Peter. "We have coffin clubs where folks build their own. They call 'em the 'D.I.Y. Coffin Clubs.'"

"Are you serious?"

"Very. My mum is building hers. She painted it burgundy with white hydrangea blossoms and it has a waterproof lining. Since she's quite alive still, she's put cushions on it and uses it on the porch for extra seating."

"This is interesting," said Ray. "Can you ask her to e-mail a photo?"

"Sure. You'll like her club's motto: 'Fine and Affordable Underground Furniture.'"

"That sounds like one of my jokes," said Ray. "Think your mum and her club members would mind if I used that?"

"I'll ask but I'm sure she'll be okay with it."

"How old is your mum?"

"Ninety-four. She used to fish a lot but she said this has been almost as much fun."

Ray was leaning over to stow his thermos when a movement on land caught his eye. Wetlands crowded the banks of the Loon River with the exception of one area across from where Ray had anchored the boat. This was a wide swale running uphill to one of the few buildable lots along the river. Tamaracks crowded the rocky ditch until up on higher ground hardwoods took over.

Raising his binoculars, Ray studied figures he could see moving along the tree line with chain saws. Given that logging is one of the economic drivers of the northwoods, he wasn't surprised. But as he watched the trees fall, he realized that whoever was logging the area wasn't cutting pine trees—they were harvesting birches.

The devastation on Lew's property came to mind immediately. Ray watched for another minute, focusing in on the loggers. He recognized one of the young men—a kid he had bought weed from two years ago.

"Peter," said Ray, interrupting his friend's concentration on the lure he had just cast, "please sit down. I have to move the boat. Something's happening up on that hill there, and I need to get a good look."

Peter took his seat and set down the muskie rod. He threw a questioning glance at Ray, who put a finger to his lips. Keeping the outboard at a low throttle, Ray eased the boat up to one of the few docks along the river. It was a good five hundred yards from where the swale emptied onto a sandy section of riverbank.

"Tell you about it when I get back," said Ray, rapidly tying the boat to the dock and stepping out. "This shouldn't take more than ten minutes or so."

The dock ended at a path that led in the opposite direction of where the logging was happening. Ray's only choice was to hike across a section of bog. He hurried through the brush, hoping for solid footing among the tag alder until he reached firmer land. He figured out his approach as he wound his way through tamarack toward higher ground.

He knew the property: a large summer home at the very top of the hill belonged to a wealthy family from Chicago who used it only on holidays, the Fourth of July and Labor Day weekends. He doubted they knew they were losing their birch trees.

He kept going until he reached the road so that it would appear to the men cutting the trees that he had parked up there. "Yo, Lanny," he called as he walked down the driveway from the house and across an open area to where three men were busy with chain saws.

The bed of an older model blue pickup parked near the loggers was nearly full of what appeared to be four-foot sections of birch trees. Ray noted the license number and committed it to memory.

"Yo, Lanny," he called again, hoping he could be heard over the roar of the chain saws.

The rough-bearded twenty-year-old named Lanny had set down his chain saw and was having a cigarette when he saw Ray coming toward him. "Sorry, man, no weed today," he said. "This weekend, maybe. How much you want? An ounce or more?"

"None right now," said Ray. "I'm looking for work. A day here or there."

───────────

Ray was known among the dealers in the area as a frequent customer. While he limited his indulgence, he had reached an agreement with Lew that she would turn a blind eye on one condition: he not deal (a mistake he had made in his early twenties, hence the misdemeanor file), but enjoying a joint now and then kept him in good stead with a crowd Lew needed to know about.

The meth cookers, the heroin users, the coke dealers—they might be the underworld of Loon Lake and living down lanes with no fire numbers, but it was the responsibility of the Loon Lake Police to know who they were and where, if only to keep a close eye in order to protect residents of Loon Lake who indulged in less felonious behaviors.

───────────

"You guys working for Consolidated Paper?" asked Ray, pretending he didn't know they were on private property. Some bad actors among the loggers justified stealing from commercial tree farms because of the sheer size of the company investments.

"Nah, this is a one-shot," said Lannie. "I'll ask the guy we're working for if he can use someone. I thought you were busy guiding all summer."

"I wish," said Ray, turning down an offered cigarette. "Been so hot this past week or two. Business is slow. Got some guys from over in the Hayward area crowding in on my territory, too. That don't help."

"Know right what ya mean," said Lanny, stubbing out his cigarette and picking up his chain saw. "I'll let ya know what I hear."

"Thanks. Who'd you say's your boss on this? I might know him."

"A guy named Tom. Goes by Tommy P, and that's all I know. But he always pays cash, so I ask no questions, don't cha know. "

"Tommy P, huh. Thanks, man. I'll bet I can track 'im down."

"Well, hell. If you do, don't tell him I told ya. Know what I mean?"

"Don't mean to make you nervous, man."

"S'okay. Jes' I don't need no trouble and I do need cash."

"Yo, got it, man."

Walking back toward the road, Ray paused to study the wreckage around him: birch trees hacked off a couple feet from the ground, very different from how trees are traditionally logged whether selective logging or clear-cut.

"Hey, Lanny," hollered Ray, encompassing the view around him with a wave of one arm, "looks like a tornado blew through here. You guys coming back to trim up those stumps?"

"Nah. We got our four-footers, and that's all we're paid for."

Walking back over boggy hillocks toward his boat where Peter was waiting, Ray checked his cell phone to call Lew or Doc but he was too far from a cell tower: no service.

"Peter, my man," he said, stepping into the boat and reaching over to start the outboard motor, "sorry to do this to you but I got to get into town and find Chief Ferris. Mind if we tackle the big girls another day?"

"Business first," said Peter. "I understand. Does this have anything to do with Partridge Lodge and Chuck Pelletier?"

"I don't think so," said Ray, backing the boat quietly from the dock. He didn't want to alert Lanny that he had been seen from the water and not from Ray's random drive down a private road. "Why do you ask?"

"Before you pulled up to the dock, I could see those guys were cutting birch trees," said Peter, "and I've seen quite a bit of that happening on the NFR development land. I assumed Chuck or Gordon had contracted for it. Maybe not?"

"Maybe not, for sure. That's information I need to get to Chief Ferris before those razzbonyas disappear."

CHAPTER NINETEEN

L ew looked up as Ray walked into her office. "Hold on one
minute, Ray," she said as she raised her right hand, "I'm right
in the middle of looking over the results of the crime lab's
forensic accountant's review of invoices submitted to Peter
Bailey and recorded by Chuck Pelletier in his financial reports.
Let me finish and we'll talk."

"Nope, no way, Chief—I just caught Lanny Federson
slaughtering birch trees on private land up on the Loon River.
Right down from Camp Bron Avon."

"Are you kidding?" Lew turned away from the report she
was reading on her computer and jumped to her feet. "I know
right where you mean," she said, coming around the desk and
strapping on her holsters. "Are they still there?"

"Think so—if we hurry, we can catch 'em. Woulda called
earlier but no cell service around there. By the time I could
make a call, it was just as fast to stop here."

With Ray in the cruiser with her, Lew sped down the
county road, lights and siren off. "So this guy Lanny said he
works for a 'Tommy P,' is that what you said?" asked Lew.

"Yep. Peter said he's seen sections of birch logged on NFR
development land, too. He assumed Chuck or Maxwell had

approved it. Could be the same crew working for this Tommy P guy. I did get the number of the license plate of the pickup they were loading."

"Why didn't you say so before," said Lew, irritated. "All right, get Dispatch on your cell. Tell Marlaine you're with me and ask her to run a check on that license plate."

Minutes later Lew turned onto the private drive leading to the summer home whose backyard had recently held Lanny Federson, his two sidekicks, and the pickup loaded with four-foot sections of birch trees. None were in sight.

All that Lew and Ray could see were severed sections of dead birch, the treetops and branches scattered like broken limbs across the green swale. What remained of the stands of mature birch trees were jagged stumps—skeletal reminders of proud trees whose leaves had once shimmered under the sun.

"Wait a moment," said Lew after Marlaine returned Ray's call with the pickup owner's name and address. "Let's not check out the address until I get a search warrant. This individual may have the stolen birch on his property. I want to go in prepared."

Lew called the county judge and explained why she was requesting the warrant. "We'll have it for you shortly," said the judge, adding, "Somebody has been cutting down birch trees on the land by my hunting shack. Consider me a victim, too, Chief Ferris. Let me know right away what you find."

In less than an hour, Lew had the warrant in hand, and with Ray following her in his vehicle, she approached the address that Marlaine had given them. She drove under a faded sign reading NORTHWOODS RV HAVEN and along a two-lane dirt road fronting a shabby collection of house trailers. That was when it dawned on her that she had heard the name of the owner of the pickup before: Tom Patterson.

Yes, she thought, that's the same name as the construction contractor that Peter Bailey had said was the one forging Peter's name on invoices related to the construction of a bridge and the purchase of pumps for the Partridge Lodge Fishing and Hunting Preserve property.

Could it be the same guy? Probably not. A construction engineer would not be living in a trailer court—not in *this* run-down trailer court anyway. The Patterson name is pretty common in the northwoods, too. Has to be someone else with the same name.

She pulled into the gravel parking space alongside a well-worn trailer home with the number 3706 on a fire number in what passed for a front yard. A lean-to shed was attached to the trailer. There was no pickup in sight, but she knew from other visits to this trailer park—most often for drug busts—that residents often saved a parking fee by using the Walmart lot across the street. A pot of marigolds in desperate need of watering marked the broken cement pavers leading to the front door.

"Ray, will you please wait here while I go in? Honk if anyone pulls up, okay?"

"Got it, Chief."

Lew pulled on the handle of an outside screen door holding ripped and sagging screens. The door, squeaking, opened to a wooden door that may have been white once upon a time and that sported a dead bolt above a black hole where a doorknob had lived once upon a time. Lew knocked. Silence. She knocked again.

"Hold your goddamn horses—I'm getting dressed," shouted a female voice from inside. The dead bolt made a grinding sound and the door was yanked open. A short, pudgy woman with stringy black hair held back by a headband stared at Lew. She was wearing a short gray T-shirt over tight yoga leggings, an outfit that emphasized her plumpness. Her eyes went immediately to the document in Lew's hand.

"No," she said, shaking her head, "got no drugs here. Tom's gone. The whole damn bunch are gone. Been gone for weeks. I kicked 'em out."

"I'm not here for drugs," said Lew. "But you know what this is, don't you. I have a warrant to search the premises for stolen goods. Are you Charlene Patterson? Is your husband at home?"

"He's not my husband," said the woman. After thinking things over for a moment and with obvious reluctance she stepped back to let Lew inside.

"Thank you," said Lew, motioning for Ray to wait by her cruiser until she needed help with the search.

"But according to our records Tom Patterson lives here," said Lew.

"He *lived* here," said the woman. "I've filed for divorce and I'm getting my maiden name back. I'm Charlene Rotowski and I kicked Tommy out. He's gone. G.O.N.E. Gone. And I have no idea where he is—I don't want to know."

"I see," said Lew, raising her eyebrows as she asked, "And when exactly did Tommy leave?"

"For the last time? Yesterday. Only 'cause he stopped in, saying he had to get something he forgot out in the shed." Her eyes turned sly. "And guess what," she said. "After that weasel left, I went out to see what he was up to, and found out he's been hiding money from me again."

Charlene waved her hands in a gesture of futility. "I mean, goddammit, y'know? Here I am working two jobs, paying childcare for our kid, and he owes me. So yesterday after he leaves, what do I find stuck under an old tire? Twenty thousand bucks. Do you believe it?

"Do you know how much money I owe because of that goombah? I still owe for delivering Benjy and that was three years ago." She looked ready to cry.

"Where's the money now?" asked Lew. Charlene's eyes narrowed.

"Why?"

"Why? Because that's money he may have been paid for stolen goods."

"I don't think so," said Charlene. A crafty look stole through her eyes. "He said he got paid for a *special job* for that creep he does stuff for. That's how he said it: *a special job*." She sneered as she repeated his words. "Like it was different from any of the other crapola he gets himself into."

"Really?" asked Lew, walking into the living room of the small trailer. She was surprised at how neat the room was. It held a well-worn sofa, two wooden chairs with cane seats, and a cluster of children's toys stacked against one wall. The shag carpeting on the floor looked freshly vacuumed.

While Charlene might have appeared unattractive at first, given her weight and poor wardrobe choice—a short shirt over tight leggings—Lew noted that her clothes were as clean as the living room. Lew bet that whatever her two jobs, she was likely a hard worker.

"What kind of special job?" asked Lew. "He isn't in construction by any chance? Building bridges, that type of work?" Lew made an effort to sound encouraging.

"Are you kidding me? Building bridges? Tommy couldn't build a fire if he was freezing to death. No, he's been doing logging for some guys over in Minnesota and then that guy he calls 'ol Max' put him on some other project." She waved a hand and snickered. "Wait, I take back what I just said. You know what pays twenty grand?"

"No idea. That's a lot of money," said Lew.

"Meth. I'll bet you this 'ol Max' guy's got Tommy cooking meth. Like I said, he can't build a fire but you give that guy a pizza oven and he's home free."

"So where is the money now? And where do you think I can find your . . . ex. I mean Tommy. Oh, and about this Max person. Where is he? If these boys are messing with meth, I need to know. I promise I'll keep you out of it if you tell me where to find them."

Charlene stared down at her bare feet. "You know I could get hurt telling you anything."

"Or you could spend the night in jail for withholding evidence."

"Right," said Charlene in a small voice. "If I give you the money and tell you what I know, will . . . um . . ."

"Yes," said Lew before she could finish. "Anything you say or do will be kept confidential, I promise."

"I know you keep your promises," said Charlene. There was nothing snide in how she made the comment.

"And how do you know that?" Lew was curious at the woman's unexpected words of trust.

"I went to school with your daughter, Suzanne. We were both dancers out at Thunder Bay for a while, too."

"That was a long time ago," said Lew.

"Suzanne and I . . . we stay in touch so I know you're . . . reliable?" She ended her comment with a rise in her voice, questioning.

"Yes," said Lew, "I am reliable."

———————

Lew would never forget that difficult year. She was newly divorced, working a secretarial job at the paper mill, and unable to afford to send Suzanne to college. Suzanne, who at eighteen was so desperate to get a degree in accounting that she found the best paying job in the northwoods and worked it for a full year. The job? She danced at a gentlemen's club, the Thunder Bay Bar.

After a year, she had squirreled away ten thousand dollars, enough in those days to get started at the university. After that, scholarships and on-campus jobs made it possible for her to finish. Today she ran her own accounting firm in Milwaukee.

And where was her mother during that hard year? Every night that Suzanne danced, Lew waited in the parking lot for Thunder Bay to close. She was there to drive her daughter home. She was there to keep her safe.

———————

"It seems a hundred years ago," said Charlene with a sad smile. "I envied Suzanne because you were there for her. You understood. My mother thought I was a whore for dancing there. Of course when she found out how much I got paid, then she made me pay rent to live at home."

Charlene shook her head and Lew felt bad for her. She was one of those souls who could never catch a break.

"Charlene, you've said enough that you *have* to turn over the cash that Tommy hid here. I'm sorry but that's the law."

Charlene nodded. "I know. I'll get it. I hid it in Benjy's laundry hamper."

When she walked back into the living room with a soiled dark green backpack and handed it over to Lew, Lew asked, "Does Tommy know you found this?"

"Nope. Like I said, he hasn't been here since yesterday and I have no idea where he's living. I'm sure he'll try to sneak back when I'm not here. If he does, I'll play stupid: Like 'What money? What are you talking about?'

"I'll say a cable TV crew came by to inspect the place. They do that all the time, trying to catch people hooking up illegally. I'll say maybe one of those guys took it. Or I'll tell him it's there somewhere. He was drunk when he hid it so maybe he can't remember. Yeah, that's what I'll tell him."

"Think you can pull that off okay?" Lew was dubious. And worried. If there was one thing she didn't want to do, it was to put Charlene in harm's way.

"Whoa. Just you watch me," said Charlene with a vengeance.

For one fleeting second, Lew felt pity for Tom Patterson. "One more thing," said Lew. "Do you have a photo of your husband that I could borrow? Something recent?"

What she didn't say was "something better-looking than the mug shot we probably have."

"Sure. I just put our wedding photos away. Let me see what I can find."

Charlene disappeared into what Lew assumed was her bedroom. "How about this?" she asked, reemerging. She held out a photo of a couple in wedding clothes smiling happily into the camera.

"He's good-looking," said Lew, surprised to see a well-groomed, handsome man in his mid-twenties. He had dark hair and pleasant features.

"I'm not so bad, either," said Charlene, pointing to the picture of her in the photo. "Thirty pounds lighter five years ago. That helps." She rolled her eyes as if the idea of being young and slender and pretty was a pipe dream long gone.

"You're right, Chief Ferris. He is a great-looking guy, but that's his curse, too. Everything came so easy when he was a gorgeous kid that Tommy never learned how to work. That's my theory anyway. He was married before me, y'know."

"Oh?" Lew was happy to have her talking, trusting.

"Married a girl from one of the rich summer families over in Minocqua. Her dad gave him a big job in one of his companies and somehow Tommy blew it. Just lazy, I think. I met him right afterward and I thought he was just so cute, y'know."

She sighed. "I gotta tell ya, only one of us ever held a job. That wasn't so bad, really. I thought I could work and he could be a househusband. But then he started hitting me. When he pulled a gun and shot through the wall over there"—she pointed to a small hole in the wall of the tiny living room—"shot a bullet that just missed Benjy in his crib. Man, he was outta here. That was it for me."

"I don't blame you," said Lew. "Sorry to hear he has a mean streak."

"Mean and not so bright. Great-looking and dumb as a

rock. I need to shut up," said Charlene. "Some days I think I was the dumb one. Gotta tell ya, though. Now, when I date a guy, I wait a long, long time before I let him in my life. Wait till I know, really know, who the hell he is."

"Do you mind if I borrow this photo? I'd like to show it to someone," said Lew. "I'll return it soon."

"I don't think I'll need that real soon," said Charlene. "Someday, maybe. To show Benjy what his papa looked like." She gave a sad smile.

As Lew pulled the cruiser into her parking space back at the department, she asked Ray to follow her to her office. Once there, she reached into a drawer in her desk for an envelope. She slipped five twenty-dollar bills into the envelope, sealed it, and handed it to Ray.

"All the mailboxes for the trailers are located at the entrance to the trailer court. Will you please check for the one belonging to Charlene Rotowski, maybe Patterson in case she hasn't changed it on her box, which might say number three-seven-oh-six, and slip this inside? She's an old friend of Suzanne's and she loaned her some money years ago. I remembered that while we were talking . . . and keep this between us, will you, please?"

"You don't have to ask, you know that."

"Thank you."

"You are as welcome as the flowers," said Ray, tucking the envelope into his back pocket as he left.

CHAPTER TWENTY

That afternoon, Lew gathered four people around the coffee table under the big window, the sitting area she liked to use for casual meetings. Sunlight through the leaves of the oak trees guarding the courthouse dappled across the long wooden table.

Sitting in the comfortable chairs were Bruce Peters, the forensic accountant from the Wausau Crime Lab, Peter Bailey, and Osborne. The accountant's report of what he had found in his review of financial documents and expense reports from Chuck Pelletier and Peter Bailey had just begun when the office phone on Lew's desk rang.

"Chief," said the receptionist at the front desk, "Molly Pelletier is here. She would like to talk to you for just a few minutes. Okay to send her back?"

A moment later Lew's door opened and a tear-stained Molly walked in. At the sight of everyone sitting around the table, she started to back out. "Sorry, I thought you would be alone." Her voice broke and she started to cry.

Osborne was the first person to stand up, and he gathered Molly into his arms. "It's okay," he said soothingly, in an effort to comfort her. "Were you able to see your father?" He spoke softly, assuming the sight of her father's body—silent in death—had put her over the edge.

"No, that's not it," she sobbed. Lew stood up, motioning for the others to leave the room. "No, no, I don't mind if they hear this," Molly said in a quavering voice. "Maybe it'll help with your investigation."

"Are you sure?" asked Lew. Molly nodded.

"Jessie and I just met with our dad's lawyer. He said Dad was ready to sign a new will that he decided to make after he married Patti . . . but he never did. He was supposed to meet with the lawyer today."

Molly took a deep breath. "But because he didn't sign it before he died, state law says that because Patti is his wife, she gets half of everything. *Everything*." Her angry eyes raked the room. "That includes the money and antiques from my mom and dad's marriage, too."

"Are you sure about that?" asked Osborne.

"Yes. Because there is no will. So that woman gets half of what my mom wanted me and Jessie to have and half of everything my dad made over all the years of that marriage, too. The lawyer told me that the will he was going to sign protected everything he had from before the marriage to Patti—all of which, including my mom's wonderful antiques, was supposed to be Jessie's and mine. It's not fair."

"Sweetie, sweetie," said Osborne, pulling her in again. He knew better than to mention life is never fair. "On a less disturbing note—have you been able to make the arrangements for your father? Are those working out okay?"

"Yes." She dabbed at her face with a Kleenex that Lew had walked over to hand her. "That very kind priest at St.

Mary's is going to let us have the Blessed Virgin chapel. He's arranging for the ladies of the church to put flowers around the casket and . . . it'll be nice. We've invited about ten people including all the staff that his secretary said worked with him. Peter"—she looked at Peter Bailey—"you're included, too, you know."

"Thank you," said Peter, standing up. "May I take you and your sister to lunch afterward?"

"I have a better idea," said Osborne. "We'll have everyone come to my place for a nice luncheon immediately after the memorial service. I'll arrange it."

"Oh, no, Dr. Osborne," said Molly, wiping away her tears. "You already entertained us—"

"Pizza is not entertaining," said Osborne. "End of discussion—my place."

After Molly left the room and Osborne was sure she was out of earshot, he turned to the group around the table. "Poor kid," he said and shook his head.

"Now that was interesting," said Bruce. "How convenient for Wife Number Two that Chuck Pelletier died before completing his will."

"Things are bad enough without you going there," said Lew, poking him.

"Just saying," said Bruce. "After all, didn't Chuck say he saw her in the car with Maxwell earlier that morning?"

The forensic accountant looked around the table. "Are we ready for me to give you my analysis?"

"Please," said Lew, "go ahead."

When he had finished, it was Peter Bailey who said, "It's obvious to me that someone tampered with the financial reports that Chuck and I thought we were working with. It is also obvious to me that the person had to be Gordon Maxwell or someone close to him, someone skilled with Excel spreadsheets. I have a weird question and I'm sure I'm off base but . . ."

Everyone sitting around the table stared at him. "Do we know what this Patti person did before she married Chuck Pelletier? Was she employed somewhere?"

"I don't know," said Lew. "Good question. Doc, you've met her several times. Why don't you and I stop by the house to see how she's doing? Bruce told me she was able to move back in late yesterday afternoon."

During the drive over to the Pelletier home, Osborne said, "Lew, I followed up on the photo your former mother-in-law showed us, the one where she identifies Gordon Maxwell as one of the men who bought her house. I showed the photo around during coffee this morning with my buddies at McDonald's.

"Two of the guys recognized the man with Maxwell. He's the current president of the Rotary Club. Not sure if that helps, but at least we know who he was with. And I doubt that fellow has any business dealings with Maxwell or the NFR development."

"That fits. Lorraine said the other man in the photo wasn't the one with Maxell when he came to her door. After what I learned today, I want to share a picture of Tom Patterson with her. Charlene told me that before she kicked him out, Patterson was running errands for Maxwell. Could be he's the man who approached her along with Maxwell, don't you think?"

The walkway up to the front door of the Pelletier home looked the same as it had the morning Chuck died: pots of pink petunias freshly watered and the stone walkway swept clean. Lew knocked on the door.

"Sorry to barge in on you like this, Mrs. Pelletier," said Lew with an ingratiating smile, "but Dr. Osborne and I have a few more questions to run by you as we finish the paperwork on the investigation of your husband's death."

"Finish?" asked Patti. "Does that mean you know what? I mean who? I mean—"

"No, I'm afraid not," said Lew. "Frankly, right now the more we learn, the more some of us feel that his death may have been the result of an accident. But we simply are not sure."

Relief snuck across Patti's face only to be erased by an expression of curiosity. "Then, whatever I can do. Please, come in. I did get a call from that lovely man, the priest at St. Mary's Church, telling me that the service for Chuck will be in one of the chapels at eleven tomorrow morning. Chuck's daughters are taking care of everything, which is so kind of them."

"Yes," said Osborne, "I think handling the arrangements is helping them deal with the grief. Very good of you to let them take charge." He smiled, knowing full well she had had no choice. "And I spoke with Molly just an hour ago, inviting everyone coming to the service to stop at my home for a luncheon immediately following the event at the church.

"I wanted to be sure you knew in case you want to invite

anyone," he added. "I've already called Chuck's secretary, Marion, and she'll be letting the staff who are coming to the service know that they are invited to the luncheon as well.

"Oh, gosh. That reminds me," he said, looking at Lew. "I better call the Loon Lake Pub and Café and ask their catering staff to take care of things. Excuse me, will you, while I make that call?"

"Of course," said Lew. "I'll follow up with Patti while you take care of that."

Lew followed Patti into the living room of the home and sat down on an upholstered armchair across from the sofa where Patti had settled herself. "Just a few questions on details I need for my reports," she said, pulling out a small notebook.

"Certainly," said Patti.

"First, what was your full name *before* you married Chuck Pelletier? I have you down as Patricia W. Pelletier but since you've been married less than two years, I've been instructed I need to have your full name as of five years ago." Lew looked over at Patti with questioning eyes and a pleasant smile.

"Of course. Patricia W. Milligan. That was my name after my first marriage, which lasted ten years, and before that, my maiden name was Carter."

"And you were employed where?" asked Lew. "I assume you were working when you met Chuck?"

"Oh yes. I was the bookkeeper for the Bradley College Science Division. I handled the bookkeeping for all the graduate fellowships and grants received by the professors. I was there for twelve years," said Patti with pride. "Our division was the college's most prestigious."

"Oh, I'm sorry, but I've never heard of Bradley College," said Lew. "Where is that located?"

"Outside Boston. It's a small, state-run school but the Science Division is well respected for its marine biology research. They have done landmark work in the field of squid propagation." Again, the proud smile.

"Interesting," said Lew, "we don't have many squid around here."

"No, you don't." Patti laughed. It was the first spontaneous laugh Lew had heard from the woman. "Anything else you need to know?"

"Yes—do you have children from your previous marriage?"

"No. I've never had children, which is why I was hoping to get to know Molly and Jessie better. But"—she sighed—"that's going to be difficult, I'm afraid."

Osborne walked into the room. "I am so glad I called. One more hour and it would have been too late to order for tomorrow. But," he said, spreading out his hands as he spoke, "it's all set—luncheon for twenty."

"And we are set here, too," said Lew, getting to her feet and extending a hand to Patti. "Thank you for your time."

Back in the cruiser, Lew drove along the paved drive and half a mile from the Pelletier property before she pulled over. "Hold on, Doc," she said while punching in Dani's cell number. "I'm anxious to get this going.

"Hello, Dani, sorry to ruin your Saturday but I need you to run a background check ASAP. Think you can manage to do this right away?" Lew waited. "Sure, finish blow-drying your client. Twenty minutes won't make a world of difference. Please call me if you find anything significant. Wake me up if you have to. Oh, and you'll be paid time and a half for this. I appreciate it."

The call from Dani came in that evening shortly before nine. Lew and Osborne were down on his dock watching the sun dip below the pines on the far shore.

The lake had shed its late afternoon crystal blueness in favor of soft swaths of rose and peach and periwinkle blue: a lake full of sky. A lake so placid, so peaceful, that Osborne wondered, as he often did when savoring summer evenings on the dock, why life couldn't be so serene.

At the sound of the cell phone's trill, Lew tipped over her glass of iced tea.

"Don't worry about it," said Osborne, grabbing for the glass. "You talk."

"Everything she told you is accurate," said Dani, reporting from where she was sitting in front of her computer. "We're in luck, Chief. Not expecting anyone to answer, I called Bradley College and a student working late in the Alumni Office gave me the name and number of the current bookkeeper for the Science Division.

"I reached her at her home and she said Patti was let go for 'financial improprieties.' Seems she was having an affair with one of the married professors and was found to have moved grant monies from one division account into a grant program run by her lover. The college decided not to prosecute, but both Patricia Milligan and the professor were asked to leave Bradley College. That was a little over three years ago."

After Lew hung up the phone, she relayed her conversation with Dani to Osborne. Well aware that sound carries over water, she spoke in a low voice. "So, Doc, we can assume that our party can read a financial report and—"

"And help an unskilled individual make adjustments to an Excel document," said Osborne, finishing her sentence.

The two of them smiled at each other.

CHAPTER TWENTY-ONE

The church was hushed as Osborne walked down the aisle toward the small chapel on the right. Molly and Jessie were kneeling off to one side of the open casket. A vase holding yellow and white gladiolus had been set on the stairs in front of the casket. Tall candles threw a glow across the quiet features of the man with whom Osborne had shared hours in the trout stream.

Not enough time for us, my friend, thought Osborne as he knelt to pray across from Chuck's daughters.

Six pews had been set up and they began to fill within minutes of Osborne's arrival. Lew showed up, in uniform, and sat next to Osborne. "Sorry, Doc," she whispered, "I know I should dress like a civilian but I want to be ready if anything breaks. I've got a meeting with Lorraine right after the luncheon, too. I want to show her the photo I got from Charlene."

"The girls will understand," Osborne whispered back.

By the time the priest was ready to say a few words about Chuck Pelletier, the pews were crowded with people. Osborne recognized Marion Hunter, Chuck's secretary, and several of the others who had been patients of his over the years.

Peter Bailey was there and, at the last minute, Patti Pelletier walked in to take the last seat in the rear pew.

The service was brief, and as people filed out of the church, Marion Hunter took Osborne's arm. "Gordon Maxwell couldn't make it here to the church but he plans to attend your luncheon. He said he was working until ten this morning and he still had to relay information about Chuck's death to the NFR execs in New York City."

"You mean he hadn't told them yet?" Osborne was incredulous.

Marion shrugged. "Gordon does things his way. It wasn't my job to make that call. Sorry."

"Oh well," said Osborne with a resigned nod in the direction of Molly and Jessie. "Maxwell's presence at lunch will make a difference to the family. I'm glad he'll be able to make it."

———

Osborne's house was buzzing. The caterers had set up in the living room with people serving themselves then wandering onto the porch to eat at one of several card tables, each seating six, which Osborne had been able to rescue from his basement. After making sure that Molly and Jessie had been served and were settled to eat with Marion, her husband, and Peter Bailey, Osborne headed toward the kitchen to see if the head caterer had any questions.

He passed Patti, who caught his eye with a wave and a hello. She appeared to be having a pleasant conversation with two young men whom Osborne didn't recognize, although he knew from Marion that several of the contractors working on the construction of the lodge buildings would be coming to the service and the luncheon.

He made a mental note to introduce himself to the contractors before the luncheon was over. He wasn't interested in who they were so much as if they could offer any insight as to what Chuck might have been doing in the office the morning before he died.

As he was talking to the caterer, the back door opened and a man walked in. Spotting Osborne, he hurried over to introduce himself. "Hello, Dr. Osborne, we've not met but I'm Bill Shauder, I've been working with Chuck and Gordon on the development of the Partridge Lodge property. Mainly with Gordon recently, but I got to know Chuck, and I find it hard to believe this has happened. Where is his family? I want to offer my condolences."

"Thank you, we all feel that way," said Osborne, shepherding him toward the porch where Molly and Jessie were sitting. "What area of the development were you involved with?" asked Osborne, being polite until he could move the man into a conversation with someone else.

"The bridges. My construction firm was hired to build three bridges over the new streams," said Shauder. "Just finished the last one—or almost finished. We have maybe a day or—"

"Did you say 'bridges'?" asked Osborne, taking him by the arm as they continued to walk in the direction of the porch. After introducing him to Molly and Jessie, he waited while Bill told the young women how badly he felt for their loss. Then Osborne tapped Peter on the shoulder.

"Peter, you must know Bill Shauder," said Osborne. "He

said he's been building the bridges over the Partridge Lodge streams." Peter looked up surprised. "I've heard the name. . . ."

"We met a year ago, I believe," said Bill, graciously, extending a hand to Peter, who was getting to his feet. "You're from New Zealand, aren't you? Where the trout are as big as our muskies." He chuckled.

"That's right," said Peter. "I'm the designer for the development. Say, I've been meaning to give you a call. Chuck and I had planned to speak about this first, but"—he looked at Bill with a grimace—"we never had the chance. You report directly to Gordon, correct?"

"That's correct. Is there a problem?"

"Just a misunderstanding," said Peter. "As I'm sure you know, Chuck was handling all the financials on the development. He mentioned to me that the project invoices he was getting from your man, Tom Patterson, were somewhat alarming in terms of cost increases. Maybe you and I can discuss this later?"

"Certainly," said Bill. "You have an extra chair here. Mind if I join you?"

Peter looked over at Jessie, Molly, and the Hunters. "These folks don't need to hear business right now."

"No, go ahead, please," said Molly. She had set down her fork and was listening. "Dad had mentioned there were issues with the bridge construction. He was frustrated that he didn't have control over those projects, since they were one of the most costly elements in the development planning. None of my business but I know it was on his mind. . . ."

Shauder was shaking his head. "I'm sorry to hear that because I went out of my way to be sure every penny was accounted for. Gordon told me he was overseeing the bridges himself since he had more experience with bridge construction and the legalities involved. He said building in Florida had been a nightmare and quite the learning experience.

"But going back to what you just said, Peter, I've never heard of a Tom Patterson. Are we discussing the same projects?"

"Excuse us," said Peter, sounding alarmed and setting his napkin on the table. "Doc, do you mind if we use your bedroom for a few minutes?"

"Go right ahead," said Osborne. The two men walked through the living room and into the bedroom. They closed the door. A few minutes later, Bill Shauder came out. "Need anything?" asked Osborne. He had taken Peter's seat at the table, ready to chat with his guests.

"Some answers," said Shauder in a grim tone. "Be right back. I have some papers in my car that Peter should see. Back in a second."

He hadn't been gone two minutes when a new person opened Osborne's rarely used front door and walked onto the porch: a short man in a business suit, his black hair standing so high on his head that it seemed to add three inches to his height.

The man hadn't gone ten feet before Jessie let out a small scream. She stiffened as the blood drained from her face.

The table where she was sitting with Osborne and the others was at the far end of the porch—far enough from the front door that the newcomer hadn't heard or noticed her reaction. The man walked past two other tables on the porch, where people were sitting, and was stepping through the doorway into the living room when Molly grabbed her sister by the shoulders. "What's wrong? Do you need a Heimlich?"

"No, no." Jessie shook her head. "That's the man who grabbed me at the airport. The man who kissed me."

"He— Who is that man?" asked Molly of the people sitting at the table.

"Gordon Maxwell," said Marion.

"The man who worked with my father?" Molly sounded incredulous. She was on her feet before Osborne could put a hand on her shoulder.

"Let me handle this," he said.

Osborne headed into the living room after Maxwell. Stopping to watch as Maxwell neared the group where Patti was standing and chatting, he saw Maxwell walk up behind Patti and, turning to one side, nudge her in the back. It was a gesture only someone watching carefully might have seen. She turned. Her eyelids drooped seductively and a slight smile crossed her face before she returned to her conversation.

Osborne remained where he was, watching. Molly, ignoring his instruction, had followed him into the living room and was standing silently beside him. Osborne was sure she had seen the nudge.

The two of them stood there, not moving, saying nothing, just watching as Maxwell picked up a plate at the caterer's stand. He was serving himself when Bill Shauder, a black leather briefcase tucked under his right arm, rushed in the back door and hurried to the bedroom. If he saw Maxwell, he gave no indication. And Maxwell, helping himself to mashed potatoes, did not see Shauder.

Molly turned to follow Shauder into the bedroom. Osborne reached into his shirt pocket for his cell phone. "Lewellyn," he said, turning toward the wall and covering his mouth, "you better get here fast."

"I'm parking as we speak," she said. "What's going on?"

"Tell you when you get here. Hurry."

CHAPTER TWENTY-TWO

Lew walked into the bedroom just as Bill was laying out documents on the bed.

"I see Gordon Maxwell is in the other room," she said as she closed the door behind her.

"S-s-h," said Osborne. He took her aside while Peter and Bill were conferring. Glancing over her shoulder as she leaned to listen to Osborne, Lew saw Molly, her eyes intent on the four people in the room, standing in one corner, listening.

"Maxwell is the man who grabbed Jessie at the airport," said Osborne in a low voice. "He walked in less than ten minutes ago. Jessie is pretty upset."

"And I'm upset," said Molly, overhearing Osborne. "That man may think it's nothing to just grab and kiss a woman, but he's wrong. Chief Ferris, you have to do something."

"Take it easy," said Lew. "Molly, this isn't the only issue I have with Mr. Maxwell. Is Jessie okay for the moment?"

"I think so, but that's no reason not to—"

"Sorry to interrupt but, Chief Ferris, you need to hear this," said Peter from across the room. "Bill and I have just compared invoices on the bridge construction throughout the

Northern Forest Resorts projects and it's clear that someone has committed fraud."

"Fraud? Try out-and-out theft," said Shauder. He introduced himself to Lew and said, "Chief Ferris, my construction firm was hired to build or repair three bridges over new trout streams designed by Peter. I was told in a private meeting with Gordon Maxwell to submit my invoices for the supplies and manpower to him directly. That is what I have been doing."

"Okay," said Lew, "where is the problem?"

Peter stepped in to say, "From the beginning *my* understanding was that I should receive *all* invoices on construction whether lodge buildings or otherwise. I was to then submit those to Chuck Pelletier. Chuck was in charge of the finances for the entire development.

"What Bill and I have just learned is that the invoices that Bill submitted were altered to increase costs substantially. Also, they were submitted to me not by Bill but by someone by the name of Tom Patterson."

"And I have never heard or met such an individual," said Bill. "He certainly does not work for me."

"Are you saying an intermediary between Gordon Maxwell and you, Peter, falsified the financial figures?"

"Not only that but Chuck and I authorized payment based on those invoices. That's what had Chuck so worried: those costs had gone over my estimates by several million dollars."

"Bill," asked Lew, "were you paid for your firm's work?"

"Yes but for the amounts I submitted—nothing more. And, interestingly enough, the invoices from this Patterson fellow show payments are to be made to a firm I've never heard of."

"How long has this been going on?" asked Lew.

"That's odd, too," said Peter. "The fraudulent paperwork is on one bridge only, which is the third and final one that Bill's crew has been working on."

"And what is weird about that," said Bill, "is that all that was needed on that bridge was reinforcing the existing culverts, which is a very small job." Osborne could see Bill was looking distressed, as if he were the one being accused of falsifying the invoices.

Lew reached over to put a hand on Bill's arm. "Before you hyperventilate, Bill, let me ask Peter to call this Mr. Patterson," she said. Then she turned to Peter and did just that. "Can you call this Patterson person and ask him to meet me in my office in an hour?" she asked him.

"I would be happy to, but I have no contact information for the guy," said Peter. "Gordon handled that communication and I have had enough going on with all the other contractors, I didn't have any reason to talk to the guy until this."

"What about when he turned in his invoices?" asked Osborne. "Did you ever question him?"

"I have never seen the guy," said Peter. "Those invoices always came in over the weekend and were slipped into Chuck's in-box without me having anything to do with them. *Except that my name was forged on those to indicate I had approved them.*"

"Okay," said Osborne, "let's ask Maxwell for Patterson's number. He's in the other room. Chief, do you want me to ask him for it?"

"No, Doc, let me do that," said Lew.

"Okay, but why don't I check with Marion, too, in case she has a number," said Osborne.

"Good," said Lew. "Ask her if she's met Patterson, too."

———————

Osborne was about to leave the room when Molly, who had been listening from where she stood in the corner behind Osborne, spoke up. "Before you go, Dr. Osborne, I need to check on Jessie. And while I'm up, I'd like to use the bathroom. Can you steer me in the right direction?"

"The guest bath is that way," said Osborne, pointing as Molly headed out of the room. "And if it's occupied, there's another one downstairs."

After she left, Osborne said, "Chief, several of the other contractors working on the development are among the guests still on the porch. After I ask Maxwell for the phone number, do you have any problem with my asking those contractors a few questions? I'd like to know if they saw or heard anything unusual in the days or weeks before Chuck died."

"Go right ahead," said Lew. "I have a few more questions for Bill, too."

Osborne walked into the living room with Peter, who pointed out three men who owned firms involved with the construction of the lodge buildings. Determined to get the phone number from Maxwell, Osborne looked for him first, but the man was nowhere in sight.

"He said he had to get something from his car," said one of the caterers standing by the table holding desserts. "Said he'd be right back and to hold a piece of cake for him."

While waiting for Maxwell, Osborne decided to check

with the three men who Peter had pointed out as being involved with the lodge construction. The first two he questioned insisted that they had seen or heard nothing unusual.
They also denied that they had been by Chuck's office that
morning.

The third man mulled over Osborne's question before an-
swering. "Now that you mention it, Dr. Osborne, I did see
something peculiar. I had stopped by the office that morning
and after chatting with Marion, I got myself a cup of coffee
for the road and a doughnut. When I was leaving, I walked
through the covered garage where some of us park in bad
weather and ran into this sketchy-looking guy poking around
the two cars parked there. One was Chuck's SUV, the other
Marion's Mini Cooper.

"I asked him what he was looking for and he said a tire
jack. When I suggested that he check inside for help, he said
he would."

"Any chance you know the guy?" asked Osborne.

"Yeah. I mean, I don't *know* him, but I've definitely seen
him before. A local. About a year ago, he applied to work for
me. The dude does some logging around the area. A real loser
type, goes by 'Tommy.' That's as much as I know."

Molly stood waiting outside the bathroom. When the door
opened and out walked the wife of one of the contractors,
Molly smiled and said, "My turn." She entered and closed the
door behind her. Moments later, while washing her hands and
then drying them on one of the hand towels set out for guests,
she leaned forward to peer out the window over the sink.

She could see the backyard and a small screened-in porch attached to the garage. Figures could be seen moving behind the porch screens. Molly watched as the figures, in shadow, appeared to embrace. They held still for a long moment. Molly smiled, imagining the couple must be Marion and her husband or maybe one of the other couples—a contractor and his wife, perhaps—who had been so kind to come to the memorial service for her dad.

Then the figures parted and walked out of the porch into the backyard toward Osborne's house. Molly's mouth dropped open. She watched in stunned silence as the man and woman touched fingers for a brief second before moving forward.

The couple? Gordon Maxwell and Patricia Milligan Pelletier.

Molly burst into Osborne's bedroom where Lew, Bill Shauder, and Peter Bailey were ending their discussion. Osborne walked in behind her and was about to ask Lew if she had been able to get Patterson's phone number from Maxwell when he saw Molly waving her arms for him to close the door and for everyone to hear what she had to say.

"You won't believe this," she said in a loud whisper. "I just saw Gordon Maxwell and my stepmother kissing out back. Now I know she *was* having an affair. Dad was right!"

"Are you sure he wasn't just offering her support?" asked Osborne. But even as he spoke, he knew the truth.

"Don't, don't . . ." warned Molly, speechless with anger as she waggled a finger at Osborne.

"Molly, I believe you," said Lew. "And I know that man accosted your sister. But you need to pull it together. You need to calm down. Now."

Lew was very adamant that Molly shut up, which surprised Osborne. He was thankful she did. If she had been one of his daughters, he doubted he would have been able to control her.

"Take a seat on the bed, please," Lew said, sitting down. "I have something to tell you." She reached for Molly's arm to pull her down beside her as the three men watched in silence.

Molly yanked her arm away and turned her back for a long moment. Then she sat, shoulders hunched. "All right. What." She stared at Lew.

"Everyone has to keep this in confidence," said Lew, her eyes connecting with each person in the room. "I am building a case against Gordon Maxwell and whoever this Tom Patterson is—for fraud and more—possibly murder."

"Don't forget my stepmother." Molly's voice was grim.

"Right now I know from Dani's research that Maxwell managed to weasel out of fraud charges in Florida so I can't let him know that I'm on to him yet. What I have just learned from Bill and Peter is that he has been working a similar scam here. This Tom Patterson character, the falsifying of the bridge expenses, and the use of an unfamiliar firm to receive those payments—it's all a front for embezzling from the Partridge Lodge development project.

"But I cannot walk out of this room and arrest him yet."

At the flash from Molly's eyes, Lew said, "I need twenty-four hours is all. I need time to document everything and sit down with our district attorney and the judge to get a warrant for the arrest of Gordon Maxwell. Does everyone here under-stand this? Do you agree to say nothing until I can move for-ward?"

Everyone, including Molly, nodded in agreement.

"And, Peter," said Lew, "I repeat, stay safe. You are a key witness."

———————

As the guests started to leave, Lew poured herself one last cup of coffee from the caterer's large coffee urn. Gordon Maxwell was standing nearby in conversation with one of the contrac-tors. Osborne started toward him but Lew waved him off.

"Excuse me, Mr. Maxwell," said Lew, "we haven't met. I'm Chief Lewellyn Ferris with the Loon Lake Police. I have a question for you. I need to reach your colleague Tom Patter-son. Can you give me his phone number, please?"

Setting down the plate of cake that he was holding, Max-well reached into the side pocket of the suit coat he was wear-ing and pulled out a cell phone. He clicked it on and studied it for a long minute. "Darn," he said, "I was sure I had Tom in here. But this is a new phone and I haven't transferred all my contacts. Sorry about that.

"Do you have a card, Chief Ferris? I can find the number later and give you a call tomorrow. How's that?"

"Just fine," said Lew. "Incidentally, I believe you bought a piece of property from a friend of mine recently."

"Not sure where you got that information," said Maxwell, looking irritated and, plate in hand, turning away, as if their conversation was over.

"The property is an older home on the lake channel a few

miles from here," said Lew, raising her voice. "You offered quite a bit less than the property was assessed at. I'm curious how you arrived at that figure."

Maxwell stared at her before saying in a condescending tone, "I don't think any of my business should be a concern of yours."

Osborne, listening from a few feet away, had to smother a smile. The guy was getting into dangerous territory.

"I'm also curious as to why you have not yet provided any of the signed paperwork necessary to record the sale. In fact, I have also learned that you are in the process of reselling that property to Northern Forest Resorts for ten times what you paid the original owner."

"How do you know that?" asked Maxwell, surprised.

"It's in the e-mails on Chuck Pelletier's laptop."

"*It is?*" said Maxwell, taken aback. He recovered quickly. "You know," he said with a dismissive wave of his hand, "I don't have time for this. Lady, that's how real estate is done. Fact of life—people always get less than they expect. Not my problem. Sorry."

He turned back to the contractor, whose mouth had dropped open as he listened to the exchange.

Lew signaled Osborne with her eyes and they walked onto the porch, now empty of guests except for Molly and Jessie.

"Give me a few hours," said Lew to the two young women. "Then Doc and I want to talk to you later. Back here for leftovers if that's okay."

"I told Jessie what I saw," said Molly with an edge of defiance.

"Fine," said Lew. "I have no problem with that but you need to know more before you do or say another word." She leaned forward to whisper, *"You must not compromise this investigation. Do I make myself clear?"*

It wasn't a question and the girls knew it. "So here at Doc's later?"

The two heads nodded.

CHAPTER TWENTY-THREE

On her way back to the police station, Lew saw that she had time to stop by the house where Lorraine was staying with her friend, Gloria. The two women were sitting in front of the television set watching a game show when Lew got there.

"Any news from the buyer of your property?" Lew asked as she sat down on a small couch beside her former mother-in-law.

"Not a peep," said Lorraine, resignedly. "Do you know more? My home is gone, isn't it?"

"Let's not jump to conclusions," said Lew. "The fact you don't have a formal bill of sale yet may mean the deed hasn't been submitted to the Register of Deeds, which means it is not yet official. I'm hoping to prevent that from happening, so keep your fingers crossed."

————————

The brief conversation Lew had had with a clerk in the Register of Deeds office earlier that day had been helpful. They looked up Lorraine's property records and nothing had yet been changed. "You won't believe how sloppy people are when it comes to registering deeds," the clerk's assistant had said. She clarified that with no new deed registered, the sale of a piece of property might be challenged.

Lew was operating on the vague hope that whoever it was that had approached Lorraine might be attempting to forge her signature on an official bill of sale. That whoever it was might be the same party forging Bill Shauder's name on invoices. And that whoever it was might be the individual known as Gordon Maxwell.

Lew leaned over to show Lorraine the photo she had borrowed from Charlene. "Does this man look familiar?"

Lorraine took the framed photo from her and studied it. "Yes. That's the other real estate agent who made me sell my house. So handsome and that's his wife?"

"Lorraine, I'm not interested in his wife. I want to know if you've seen this man before."

"Yes, I'm sure that's the other man who came to my house with the one who has the big hair. This man had the plat book that showed the lot lines for my property. He's the one said he knew the county was going to condemn my property. He seemed to know what he was talking about. . . . They both did."

The old woman gave a weak smile. "Guess I'm not very smart, am I?"

"Don't beat yourself up, Lorraine," said Lew, getting to her feet. "Anyone would have believed those two. But if you're sure, then this is just what I need to know.

"So say your prayers, Lorraine. Those guys might think they're smart but—you and me—we got their number. This might work out yet." She gave the old woman an encouraging smile and a hug.

Back in her office she placed a call to the district attorney and the judge, both of whom she was able to reach at home. After sharing the information she had from Bill Shauder and Peter Bailey, they assured her an arrest warrant would be ready in the morning.

Her next call was to the DNR official working on the theft of the birch trees. She described the scene on the private land that Ray had shown her and encouraged him to track down "a sometime-logger who goes by 'Tommy' Patterson. You won't find him at the address in the phone book," she said. "He's going through a divorce and doesn't live there anymore. I suggest you have your people try the bars."

Then she drove out to Osborne's. Letting herself in the back door, she could hear voices—Osborne's and two loud female ones. She headed for the porch. Three people looked up as she walked in and Lew could see Molly and Jessie were tense. She hadn't even gotten to "hello" before Molly said, "Gordon Maxwell murdered my dad, Chief Ferris. I know he did. He might not have been there, but he's the reason my dad is dead."

"You may be right, Molly," said Lew, sitting down on the porch swing across from her. "But here's what I have to deal with and I want you to listen hard because accusing is one thing, proving is another."

Molly opened her mouth to say something but Lew raised a hand to stop her, saying, "Wait. Please.

"First thing in the morning, I am declaring Gordon Maxwell a 'person of interest' in your father's death. At the same time, I will have a warrant for his arrest for attempting to defraud the Northern Forest Resorts and their Partridge Lodge development. What you two need to understand are two things: first, I have no proof *yet* of Maxwell's involvement in your father's death."

Again, Molly opened her mouth and Lew shut her down. "But I am convinced he is involved. You do not have to worry about that. My investigation is ongoing and I promise to keep you updated.

"What concerns me right now is the difficulty I run into proving Maxwell's efforts to commit fraud, if not embezzlement. The legal twist that makes that difficult is that we—meaning the Loon Lake Police and the district attorney—have to prove that there has been an *intent* to defraud the parent company."

"I don't understand," said Molly.

"Maxwell can allege that he was simply bad at doing business. Hiring the wrong people, submitting error-filled invoices, and so on. And he has the money to hire lawyers skilled at proving that he didn't know he was doing the wrong thing. Happens all the time in fraud cases.

"I was just told that by our district attorney, who is a smart guy and, by the way, married to Doc's daughter, Erin. Mark is the DA's name and he has been down this road before so he knows."

"Is this true?" asked Osborne. "Are you saying that Maxwell's defense could be that he was too stupid to handle the finances correctly?"

"He can also allege—now that Chuck is dead and not here to defend himself—that it was all Chuck's fault. That it has been Chuck who made critical errors in reporting the finances and making the payments."

"Excuse me," said Jessie. "I'm not the math whiz my sister is but I am wondering how much money we're talking about?"

"We think ten million dollars or more may have been embezzled from the Partridge Lodge accounts using this Tom Patterson and his supposed construction firm as a front through which Maxwell laundered the kickbacks.

"Meanwhile, Maxwell has had another scam going. He bought property from at least one elderly, financially naive individual whose land abuts the Partridge Lodge development for a significantly distressed price. He appears to be in the process of reselling the same property to Partridge Lodge for five hundred seventy-five thousand dollars."

"What do you mean 'in the process' and whose land are we talking about?" asked Osborne. "How did you find this out?"

"Dani discovered the potential sale of the property to the Partridge Lodge development in Chuck's e-mails—an e-mail that arrived after Chuck's death. An e-mail sent for two reasons: first, to make it look like Maxwell had no idea that Chuck had been killed; and, second, to give the proposed land sale the appearance of a legitimate transaction.

"I happen to know about the property in question because it belonged—or, I hope, still belongs—to my former mother-in-law. She came to me for help when a good friend convinced her she had been bamboozled. Lorraine is a dear person, but she is in her late eighties, hard of hearing, and"—Lew sighed—"not very bright.

"Maxwell's plan, I think, is that a new CFO will replace Chuck and he'll be able to slip the purchasing of that land from the company he is using as a front, which is the same company that has been receiving payments based on the forged invoices."

"So he has made millions of dollars doing this?" asked Molly.

"So far. If I can't stop him, if the courts can't stop him, he may make more. Or"—Lew pressed her lips together in a grim smile—"he may decide to take what he has, and skedaddle like he did in Florida."

"Stopping the fraud is in the hands of the lawyers," said Lew. "I am convinced he will be stopped but it will take time. As I said, Gordon has the resources to hire expert lawyers to make his case that he did not commit fraud intentionally. Our DA and his staff will have their hands full and it will take time to fight this. I hate to say this but it's a little like the Loon Lake Market battling Walmart. Not hopeless but not easy."

Osborne scooted his chair forward. Elbows on his knees and his hands clasped in front of him, he said, "Look, Molly and Jessie, the way I see it, here's the problem: you can let your anger with Gordon Maxwell take over your life or you can have confidence in Chief Ferris and her investigation—and in the legal team here in Loon Lake.

"Now it may take months, even a year, to nail Maxwell. He's a gifted con man; he knows what he's doing and how to do it.

"I know this will be hard," said Osborne, keeping his eyes on the two sisters, "but I'm sure, very sure, that your father would agree with me: let go of this, get on with your lives. *Do not let avenging your father's death become an obsession.*"

"Doc is right," said Lew. "If you wake to this every morning, you'll never move on. You'll never have a life—marry, have children."

Jessie had tears running down her cheeks. "So what are we supposed to do? Give up?"

"Absolutely not," said Lew. "I want you to feel confident that justice will be done. Your father's death will not go unpunished."

Molly, who had been listening and saying nothing, put an arm around her sister's shoulders. "It's okay, Jessie. We should let Chief Ferris take care of this. Dr. Osborne is right."

Molly accepted their advice with such equanimity that Osborne was surprised. He had expected more argument, more anger, more tears. Relieved on the one hand, he couldn't get over a gut feeling that Molly was holding something back.

After the girls had driven off, Osborne turned to Lew. "You must be exhausted. Ready for an early bedtime?"

"Yes, but not here, Doc. I need to be at my place. You're welcome to join me but tomorrow is Monday and I want to be in the office by six at the latest. I want that warrant and I want Gordon Maxwell under arrest. He'll make bail, I know. But he will have to stay in this jurisdiction—no more flying off to Las Vegas and who knows where else."

With that, she sighed. "At least it's a start. I've promised the girls. Let's hope I can do the job." She gave Osborne a sad smile. "Wish me luck."

CHAPTER TWENTY-FOUR

Hey, Jess," said Molly, glancing over at her sister sitting in the passenger seat of their rental car, "it's been a long day. I need time to decompress. So I'm going to drop you off at the motel but I need to drive a little, maybe stop somewhere and have a beer. Okay with you? I'll be back in an hour."

"Sure. I'm exhausted and I still need to wash my hair. I'll leave the door unlocked."

Molly pulled into the parking lot of the Loon Lake Motel and waited while Jessie grabbed her purse and jacket. She watched her sister open the door to their room and go inside. She checked her watch. It was after nine.

She wasn't sure when the blood-black animal had moved into her gut: Was it when she learned that Patti had been in the SUV with Maxwell and her father was sure they had tried to kill him? Was it when she saw Maxwell and Patti walk into Dr. Osborne's yard after embracing and touch hands? Or was it when Chief Ferris said it might take years to convict Maxwell of fraud, of her father's murder?

Didn't matter: she knew what she had to do.

Minutes later she pulled into one of the half dozen parking spaces at the private hangar. The tiny main terminal for the Loon Lake Airport was dark. Molly wasn't surprised. Commercial planes and even most of the private jets used the Rhinelander/Oneida County Airport. Pilots like herself, owners of single-engine aircraft, liked the convenience of the small airports—less air traffic and less expensive.

She pressed in the code for the side door and let herself in. She walked over to her plane, climbed inside, and reached for her tools. Outside her plane, she walked over to the six-seater Beechcraft Bonanza that she knew belonged to Gordon Maxwell.

Before she got started, she stood dead silent, making sure no mechanic was working late. She peered all around. No one else was in the hangar. She scanned the overhead steel beams and along the top edges of the outer walls. No surveillance cameras. But she hadn't expected any, not in a small rural town like Loon Lake where the only surveillance cameras were likely to be in the two public library restrooms.

The task was so simple, she found it hard to believe it would work. But she knew it would. Was it easier than altering and forging an invoice? Sure. Was it easier than bludgeoning a man on the side of the head? Sure. Was it something she could live with for the rest of her life? Molly smiled.

She was back at the motel in half an hour. Jessie was in her pajamas and blow-drying her hair in front of the bathroom mirror. When her hair had dried and she climbed into the queen-size bed they were sharing, she snuggled up to her older sister. "I hope I can sleep tonight," she said with a sigh.

Molly wrapped her arms around Jessie's shoulders and gave her a hug. "I hope you can, too, Jess. I'm pretty sure I will.

"Say, you know what? How about tomorrow morning we

go get Dad's fly rods and his fishing vest? Chief Ferris and Dr. Osborne and Peter said they'd take us fly-fishing later this week. And Mom always said the secret to a happy life is planning ahead."

Jessie hugged her back. "Do you think that Ray guy might come, too? He's cute."

Molly punched her in the arm and said, "Silly girl, go to sleep now." And the two of them giggled.

CHAPTER TWENTY-FIVE

Lew's personal cell phone rang shortly after 2:00 a.m. As she climbed over Osborne to scramble for the phone, she said, "Sorry, Doc, but it's your own fault. If you hadn't insisted on following me out here to the farm, you could be getting a good night's sleep."

As she raised the phone to her ear, all she heard at first was heavy breathing. Thinking it was a crank call from someone trying random phone numbers, she was about to click off when a female voice whispered between labored breaths: "Chief Ferris?"

"Charlene? Is that you?" Lew was sure she recognized the caller. "Are you okay?"

"He's here. In the shed. Looking for the money. I'm hiding in Benjy's closet. Can you hear me?"

"Yes. I'll be right there. Is he armed?"

"Not sure. He's real angry for sure. Told him he can't find the money 'cause he was drunk when he hid it and I don't know where it is—"

A sudden crash and the wail of a child were followed by the phone clicking off.

"Doc, call nine-one-one and tell Dispatch to reach Officer

Donovan. Emergency," said Lew, grabbing her pants. "He's on duty tonight and I need him to meet me at the Northwoods RV Haven camp on Lincoln Street at house number three-seven-oh-six ASAP. Might be a hostage situation and Patterson could be armed." She grabbed a shirt and shoes.

"I'm coming, too."

"I can't wait for you, Doc. Whatever you do, don't approach without a signal from me."

"Got it. Don't worry and be careful." But Lew was out the door, still buckling her holsters, before he had finished talking.

At the trailer court, Lew hadn't gone far down the two-lane road between the trailers when she saw a red pickup parked in front of Charlene's place. Officer Donovan was waiting in his squad car on the other side of Charlene's short driveway with his lights off. He blinked the lights once to let her know he saw her.

As Lew pulled up, she could see birch logs piled haphazardly in the bed of the pickup. A blue tarp, which had been thrown over the load, had slid halfway off, exposing the cargo.

Lew got out of her cruiser and motioned for Donovan to follow her. A light shone through an opening in the small shed to one side of the trailer home and she could see a man down on all fours rummaging through boxes. As she approached, he grabbed a tire and threw it behind him.

"Freeze, Patterson," she said, holding her Sig Sauer in both hands and pointing it at Patterson. "You're under arrest."

"What the hell—" The kneeling man twisted sideways to stare up at her. "Get outta here. This is my house."

"No it's not," screamed Charlene, who rushed through the screened door toward Lew. "He's wrecking all my stuff, Chief Ferris," she cried. "He smacked Benjy." She was hysterical.

"Calm down, Charlene," said Lew from where she was standing with her gun pointed at Patterson. "Officer Donovan, help her out, would you please?"

"What?" The man had got to his knees and was sputtering. "Why are you arresting me in my own house?"

"You're under arrest for the theft of birch logs from private property," said Lew.

"Fine," said the man. "Let me find my money first." He turned back toward the stack of tires.

"Give it up, Patterson," she said. "I have your money."

Tommy Patterson's jaw dropped as he turned to look at the police officer standing in the driveway. "What did you say?"

At the police station, Lew and Osborne faced Patterson as they prepared to interrogate him together. "This is being recorded, Mr. Patterson, while Dr. Osborne and myself ask you a few questions," said Lew. "At any time, you are welcome to call your lawyer."

"Can't afford it," said Patterson with a wave of his hand. "You got all my money. But why is *he* here?" asked Patterson, pointing a finger at Osborne and sounding confused to see a man who had checked his teeth during school exams seated across from him in the Loon Lake Police Station.

"Dr. Osborne is one of my deputies," said Lew. "He's good at asking questions that are different from the ones I ask. Speaking of questions—how long have you been cutting and stealing birch logs?" Lew waited while Patterson stared down at his knuckles, which were resting on the table. His mouth moved.

"Don't mumble, answer me," said Lew. "Look, Mr. Patterson, the more honest you are, the less the penalties you'll face. Now we've got the stolen logs in your truck and I have a witness who spoke with friends of yours who said they were cutting the birches for you, that you were paying them. So tell me—who buys these from you?"

"A guy in White Bear Lake over in Minnesota," said Patterson. "I got his name in my phone but you took my phone."

"Yes, I did," said Lew. The phone was sitting on a counter along the wall and as if it had heard itself mentioned, it rang. Patterson looked over at it. "Can I answer?"

"No." Lew waited for the ringing to stop. Then she got up and walked over to pick up the cell phone. She read the caller ID before setting the phone back down.

"Who was it?"

Lew ignored him. "Got another question for you first. How much do you get for a load of birch logs, Mr. Patterson?"

"The name is Tom," he said wearily, "five hundred bucks. Then I pay my guys twenty-five or thirty each depending. What'll I serve, Chief—a couple months? Can I get out on Huber?" He referred to the Wisconsin law that lets jail inmates hold jobs while incarcerated.

"How many loads have you delivered to this man in White Bear Lake?"

"Ten."

"So you've made five thousand dollars?"

Patterson shrugged. "Yeah—'bout that."

Lew got up and left the room. Osborne, seated beside her, watched Patterson's face while Lew was gone. Chewing on a fingernail, he looked worried.

Lew walked back into the room and tossed a filthy dark green backpack onto the table in front of Patterson. "What's inside, Tom?"

He hesitated, looked away, then said, "My money."

"More than five thousand dollars."

Silence.

"What job paid you twenty grand? . . . And why did you just receive a phone call from Gordon Maxwell?"

"I did?" Patterson did not look surprised. "Maybe 'cause I do special jobs for him sometimes? Nothing wrong with that."

"No, there isn't," said Lew. She glanced over at Osborne, signaling it was his turn.

"What kind of jobs, Tom?" asked Osborne, making sure he sounded friendly.

"Oh, office stuff mostly. Maybe deliver memos to the main office from his house where he likes to work. Maybe check out some pieces of property for 'em. He buys old cabins and stuff. Investments, y'know."

"Investments?"

"Sure. See, Maxwell is one of those brilliant guys who sees money where the rest of us see trees." Patterson had scooted forward on his chair and grinned at his own joke. "So I've been learning from him and one of these days, he said he'll make me a partner.

"That guy has made millions and he's gonna make millions more. All you gotta do is watch. Those boys in New

York, I tell ya they don't know what they're sitting on but Gordy does."

"And he's going to cut you in?"

"Yep. Been helping him out and our first deal is almost done."

Now Patterson sat back with a smug smile. During Lew's questioning, Osborne had recognized him as one of the local men who attended Loon Lake High School athletic events wearing his letter jacket from a bygone era: his own glory days.

"When did you start working with Chuck Pelletier?" asked Osborne. "I understand you own a small construction company that has done some bridge work out on some of the Partridge Lodge properties."

"Uh, not exactly," said Patterson. "I'm not sure what you're referring to." Osborne looked down at one of the forged invoices that Lew had slid across the desk.

"Well, I see here an invoice from a firm that you own for bridge work. Your signature is on it." He showed it to Patterson.

"Oh, that. That's not my company. That's one of Gordy's."

"So who got paid? You or Gordy?" Osborne used Patterson's name for Maxwell.

"Gordy, of course. Yeah, see, my job was to deliver the memos and stuff on Sunday nights when Gordy finished all his paperwork."

"What about the real estate?" asked Lew, rejoining the interrogation. "Did you help with that, too?"

"Yes, indeed," said Patterson with confidence. His face changed, as if he had just thought of something important. "That's how I made that money that you found. See, I know the area around here. I know the good lake properties and such. So I've been helping Gordy buy up some of those, see. That money's my commission." He sat back satisfied with his answer.

Lew got up and walked over to the door. "Officer Donovan, would you come in and bring that item with you, please?" She walked back to the table and sat down.

"What's the last piece of property you helped Gordon Maxwell buy?" she asked.

She had just finished asking the question when there was a knock on the door and Officer Donovan walked in.

He was wearing nitrile gloves and carrying a long, smooth piece of bleached wood shaped like a club. "Is this what you want, Chief?"

"Thank you," said Lew. "Tom, we found this on the floor of your pickup behind the driver's seat. Why don't you tell us about it?"

"What's there to tell? It's a hunk of wood I found. Thought it had an interesting shape, thought I might put it on a wall in my house someday. So?"

"Officer Donovan," said Lew, "would you please show Mr. Patterson what we see on one end of that driftwood?" The officer held the piece of wood out so everyone could see the dried blood on the club-like end.

"I'll be having this tested for DNA," said Lew. "I know what we'll learn. We'll learn that the bloodstain DNA matches that of Chuck Pelletier who was bludgeoned to death a few days ago. Do you want to tell me about it?"

Patterson said nothing. He looked like he was about to vomit.

"Let me clarify things, Tom," said Lew. "You can do a few months, maybe a year or two for theft of the birch logs. That will be in addition to years—possibly life—for the murder of Chuck Pelletier.

"Now, if you choose to tell us who buys the birch logs, the DNR may cut you a deal on that little project." She waited a beat before saying, "If you tell me that Gordon Maxwell hired you to kill Chuck Pelletier, you may have a chance to see your son graduate from college. Maybe high school, depending on how much you tell us.

"Think it over." She and Osborne stood up and left the room.

They watched through the one-way glass window as Patterson dropped his face into his hands. His shoulders shook. His forehead hit the desk and his body hung there not moving.

———————————

Out in the hallway, Lew took a photo of the driftwood and e-mailed it to Molly.

In less than a minute Molly called Lew's cell. "That's it, Chief Ferris. Where did you find it?"

"I can't say anything yet," said Lew, "but we may have found the man who killed your father. I promise to tell you more in the morning. Try to get some sleep."

———————————

Osborne followed Lew back into the interrogation room.

"Why Chuck Pelletier?" she asked Patterson after he'd sat up and wiped at his face.

"Yes, why Chuck Pelletier?" Osborne repeated Lew's question. "He was a good, kind man. Why on earth?"

"Gordon said he was in the way," said Patterson, dropping the nickname he'd been using. "Gordon said that the guy was questioning the invoices Gordon sent to him—"

"The ones you delivered?" asked Osborne.

"I guess that's what those were. He said if we got Pelletier out of the way, the next CFO would be easy to convince and we could do whatever we wanted. Gordon said that's what he did in Florida and it worked. He made ten million bucks down there."

"He lied. He left town before they could nab him for fraud," said Lew. "I would be surprised if he had ten dollars on him when he skipped. No, he lied about that and he lied telling you he'd make you a partner. You've been conned, Patterson. I think you'd better call a lawyer."

At the expression of despair on Tom Patterson's face, she said, "The public defender will work for you. I'll call her now. But know that the more honest you are, the better the law will treat you."

"I have a question, Tom," said Osborne. "How the heck did you and Gordon Maxwell connect in the first place?"

"Oh, that," said Patterson, his shoulders slumping. "You know that house he rents? It's got two hundred forty feet of frontage on Porcupine Lake and birch trees all along, just above the shoreline. I was cherry-picking those one day and he saw me—"

"Caught you, don't you mean?" asked Lew.

"Yeah, well, he made me a deal. He wouldn't report me if

I'd run a few errands for him. Then we found we got along, y'know?"

Right, thought Osborne, he knew an easy mark when he saw one. Easy mark? Hell, an idiot. A murderous idiot.

Patterson's cell phone rang again. This time Lew handed it to him. "Be careful," is all she said.

He answered, listened, and said, "Okay, I'll be there." He clicked the phone off. "That was Gordon. He likes me to drive him to the airport so that antique Corvette of his doesn't have to be parked out in the lot and get rained on. I'm supposed to pick him up at eight thirty in the morning. Said he's flying to Las Vegas with his girlfriend."

"Good," said Lew. "I'm a good driver. I'll take care of him. What's the address?"

After charging Patterson with the murder of Chuck Pelletier and following the necessary protocols, it was nearly 5:00 a.m. Osborne drove home to get a change of clothes while Lew did the same.

At five thirty that morning Tom Patterson's phone rang once more. Since the phone was in need of recharging, Lew had powered it off and plugged it in, leaving it in her office while she drove home.

Osborne and Lew both arrived back in her office shortly after six, and together, over coffee, they waited until seven when Lew could pick up the warrant for the arrest of Gordon Maxwell.

CHAPTER TWENTY-SIX

It was six fifteen that morning when Gary Geches, the mechanic in charge of supplies in the private hangar, saw the driver of a familiar low-slung sports car park in one of the few spaces next to the hangar and get out to reach in the back for a small black overnight case. His passenger, a woman, opened her own door. She walked toward the hangar carrying a pink overnight case and a large flowered purse that resembled a laundry basket.

The driver threw his keys at the mechanic and told him to drop them in the office of the manager of the main terminal. "Thanks, man," he said and kept on walking.

No tip, of course, mused the mechanic. Maxwell never tips.

He watched as the couple climbed into the small plane, the plane motored out onto the tarmac, and the pilot finished his preparations for the flight except one: the overdue equipment inspection.

The mechanic resisted the impulse to warn the woman. If he were about to fly with that goombah he would want to know the date of the plane's most recent equipment inspection, especially since every other pilot and every mechanic caring for planes using that hangar knew Maxwell's plane had not been inspected in months, knew that the plane—in housekeeping terms—was a mess.

"None of my business," the mechanic muttered to himself, repeating what Maxwell had said to him a couple months earlier when, assuming a simple oversight, the mechanic had pointed out the need for some basic maintenance on the single-engine plane.

"None of your business," Maxwell had said, adding an expletive. "You wanna work on a plane—buy your own."

Twenty minutes later Maxwell's Beechcraft Bonanza was airborne, lost from sight above a low cloud bank. The mechanic went back to checking his supply cabinet.

It was 7:30 a.m. when Lew and Osborne pulled into the driveway of the large brick home that Maxwell was renting. Lew had picked up the warrant for the arrest of Gordon Maxwell for complicity in the murder of Mr. Charles Pelletier.

The nearest door of the four-door attached garage was open—the space empty. Lew got out of her cruiser, followed by Osborne, and they walked over to peer inside the garage. The entire garage was empty.

"Uh-oh," said Lew, remembering too late that she had powered down Tom Patterson's mobile phone. Had Maxwell called to change his departure time?

She reached Dispatch and asked Marlaine to check the cell phone, which was plugged in and sitting on the file cabinet beside her desk. "I'll hold," said Lew.

Less than five minutes later, Marlaine had the disappointing news: "Hey, Tommy boy," the man's message had been, "calling to tell you I need that pickup at six a.m., not eight thirty. Gonna take Patti to Vegas and grab breakfast on the way."

There was one more message left after it had become clear to Maxwell that Patterson hadn't gotten his message for the earlier departure. "Hey, bud, forget it. Leaving the keys in the main terminal. You know the drill—get the car. And next time? Don't turn off your goddamn phone."

That was Gordon Maxwell's final voice mail.

"Chief"—Dani ran into Lew's office shortly after ten that morning—"turn on the TV!"

Lew, who had been trying to salvage her spirits after missing Maxwell and trying to convince herself he was not leaving the country, looked up, irritated. "I don't want to watch the news. Having a bad enough day already."

"Chief—turn on the television," said Dani with more authority than she thought she owned. "A small plane crashed outside of Ladysmith in the woods and it's still burning. A logger who heard the crash and ran over said he found a wallet of someone named Gordon Maxwell. A business card said he was with a company located here."

"Why didn't you say so?" asked Lew, jumping to her feet. "Holy cow."

Holding her breath, Lew stood alongside Dani as they watched the breaking news update. The second it was over, she picked up her phone to call Osborne.

"I'm driving over to the crash site right now, Doc," said

Lew. "About an hour, maybe ninety minutes, away. Want to go along?"

"Lewellyn, we were up all night. If you don't mind, you go. Call me when you know more but I have to get some sleep."

CHAPTER TWENTY-SEVEN

Bulldozers were still clearing access to the crash site when Lew arrived. Debris, blackened by fire, had been cordoned off as firefighters and paramedics picked their way through the wreckage. The local sheriff waved to Lew as she approached.

"No survivors," he said. "I don't expect the FAA or NTSB to get here for a few days, so who knows what happened. Most I can say is the plane plunged into the trees here at high speed and when it hit, the fuel tank ruptured instantly. Whoever was on board is burned to a crisp. The paramedics aren't even finding body parts. But, hell, I'm no avionics expert."

"Me neither," said Lew. "But the plane did leave the Loon Lake Airport early this morning. At least we know that much."

"Yes, we do," said a voice from behind Lew. She turned to see a familiar face as the man in mechanic's overalls extended a hand. "Gary Geches, Chief Ferris," he said, "I'm an avionics equipment mechanic and I work for the Loon Lake Airport. I saw this plane take off this morning. Hurried over the minute I heard the news. Can't say I'm surprised."

"Hi, Gary, I know you," said Lew, shaking his hand. "You went to school with my son."

"You remember," said Gary. "That was a while ago."

"It was," said Lew with a tinge of sadness in her voice. "Say, Gary, walk me through this, will you, please? Like what can cause a plane like this to go down?"

"Oh, golly," said Gary, "that's a tough one. For starters, people don't realize how dangerous general aviation is—on average three private planes crash daily, believe it or not. Sometimes pilot error, sometimes defective equipment. And sometimes—"

"You said you 'aren't surprised' by this one," said Lew. "Why would you say that?"

"Every one of us working around Maxwell's plane for the last nine months has been expecting something like this," said Gary.

"When it came to basic maintenance on his plane—the guy was a slob. A joke. Y'know, he's the type thought he was so smart that he didn't have to follow the guidelines for keeping a single-engine aircraft in operating condition.

"My opinion? He treated his plane like it was a car and the worst that might happen was a flat tire. And that is damn stupid. Chief, the minute you own a plane, you own risk."

Lew mulled that over. "Is it easy for someone to sabotage a plane like this?"

"Well, there are ways to do that. You could drill a hole in the manifest, which would cause a carbon monoxide leak. Pilot and passengers would never know. They would just pass out and that's that.

"But, Chief, only another pilot or a mechanic like me would know how to do that. And I can assure you there is no one flying or working out of our hangar who would ever think of doing such a thing."

"But if they did?"

"If they did, you'd never know. This aircraft"—he paused to let his eyes wander over the blackened debris, patches still smoking—"is decimated. Just destroyed. I'll bet you anything that wallet they found is all they'll find. Too bad, too, if only that joker had maintained it—it was a nice aircraft."

"Spoken like a true mechanic," said Lew, patting Gary on the shoulder.

"Say, Chief," he said, turning to her with a slight smile, "I still miss Jamie. He had his demons but he was a good guy. We went all through grade school and high school together. Best buds sometimes. I was there the night he was killed. And it was an accident. I hope you know that."

"Thank you, Gary," said Lew, startled to hear her son's name. "I do know that. I've always known it." She dropped her head. "I have to get back. Stay in touch, will you?"

"Hey," he said, "if you ever want flying lessons, give me a call."

"Really? You own a plane?" asked Lew.

"I own a *share* in a single-engine Piper Comanche."

"Well maintained, I'm sure."

"You betcha."

CHAPTER TWENTY-EIGHT

Did you hear the one about the guy who went to the lumber yard and said, 'I want to buy a two-by-four,'" asked Ray, lounging happily in the captain's seat on his pontoon boat. "'Sure,' said the clerk. 'How long do you want it?' Guy says, 'I want to keep it—what do you think?'" Ray waited for laughter but Molly and Jessie just looked confused.

After some thought, Molly gave a weak chuckle saying, "Okay, I get it."

He decided to try again. "Did you hear about the chameleon who couldn't change color?"

Happy to play along with what sounded like a better joke, the girls shook their heads "no" in unison.

"He had reptile dysfunction."

"N-o-o-o," groaned Jessie, though Lew could tell she was delighted.

———

Early that morning Lew and Doc had had to twist Ray's arm to get him to take his pontoon out on the lake so Peter could instruct Bruce on the long cast so popular in New Zealand.

"I know you don't fly-fish, Ray," Lew had said when he resisted, saying he had plans to hit Pelican Lake for muskie. "Oh, c'mon, Ray. Peter and I need open water and Loon Lake will be ideal. The Prairie River, the Elvoy, even the Ontonagon are too narrow for long casts. You might learn something too, y'know."

Ray was still resisting when Lew remembered to mention that Jessie and Molly would like to come along.

"Well, heck, why didn't you say so before?" asked Ray, jumping to his feet and dashing over to open his refrigerator. "In that case, you better let me pack the lunch. How 'bout egg salad sandwiches and cheese curds? When do you want to go? Do I have time for a shower? Change clothes?" He talked so fast Lew knew she'd hit a nerve.

Walking back up to Doc's house from Ray's trailer, she winked at Osborne. "Forget fishing for fish," she said. "Ray's got his priorities."

———————

Listening to Ray's attempts to charm her sister, Molly, who was reclining in a swimsuit on the padded bench along the front of the pontoon, kept her eyes closed as she let an easy grin creep across her features.

Watching from where she sat on the bench across from Molly, Lew could see the young woman was more relaxed than she had been all week. Happy even.

"So, Ray, I have one," said Jessie, bouncing up and down in the padded seat next to Ray. "What happens when frogs park illegally?"

Ray did his best to give her the dim eye before saying, "They get toad?"

Jessie pouted.

"Girl, that is one old joke," said Ray, burnishing his comedic credentials.

"Yeah, well, yours can be pretty bad, too, Mr. Pradt," said Lew, interrupting their banter. "Count your blessings, Jessie, at least he's not telling any of his off-color ones today." She stood up on the gently rocking pontoon and got ready to move to the back of the boat. "Now, girls," she said in a mocking tone, "keep an eye on that razzbonya while I check on our fly fishermen."

She smiled to herself as she walked along the deck of the pontoon. From the looks of it, Jessie had plans for Ray. Time for that young woman to have some lightness in her life, thought Lew. While it wouldn't diminish her grief over her father's death, it might help her get from one day to the next. Molly was a different case and Lew wasn't sure how to handle that one.

They had picked the perfect morning to go out on the water. Loon Lake was so calm that as the boat cruised along, Lew counted half a dozen people out on paddleboards. And for a change, kayaks outnumbered ducks.

———

It had been three days since Gordon Maxwell's plane had crashed and burned. All that the first responders had been able to salvage from the ashes was one wallet and shards of a pink overnight case. Identifying what remained of the two passengers would be Osborne's responsibility.

With help from Dani and Marion, the Partridge Lodge development secretary, he had been able to locate the dental offices where Gordon Maxwell and Patricia Milligan Pelletier had last been treated and arranged to have their most recent X-rays sent to the Wausau Crime Lab. While he had yet to match them with the skull fragments located at the site, he and Lew were confident the records would confirm the identities of the victims.

At the news of Maxwell's death, Tom Patterson had turned eager to help sort through the deception in which he had been a willing partner in hopes he might get reduced sentences for fraud and murder. His cooperation helped Peter determine that Patterson had known nothing of the actual fraud.

Once Peter confirmed that the overpriced bridge construction had, in fact, never occurred, he was able to bring on a legitimate construction firm to complete the work. Meantime, the hedge fund executives had launched a search for a new CEO and CFO to replace Maxwell and Chuck.

Though Patterson had posed as a broker helping Maxwell purchase Lorraine's property, that was his only involvement in that venture. After Peter and Marion sorted through the papers and files in Maxwell's messy office, they were able to alert Lew to the fact that a new deed to Lorraine's property had never been filed.

With that news Lew was able to connect Lorraine with a lawyer who could help restore her ownership of her home and land. The twenty thousand dollars Lorraine had received from Maxwell might have been a paltry sum for her home and land, but it took care of any legal bills connected with the fraudulent purchase.

And hours after meeting with that lawyer, Lew, along with Osborne and Ray, was happy to help the elderly woman move back into her home, plug in her television and coffeemaker, and organize her gardening tools: life as Lorraine had known it was working again.

"Lewellyn, I can't thank you enough," Lorraine had said when she got the good news, "I'm going to put you in my will as my heir to everything I own."

"No, Lorraine, you are not," Lew had said emphatically. "If you want to do something for me, you can leave all your assets to our local domestic abuse prevention team. Those social workers can use every penny to help abused families."

As she spoke, Lew could see that Lorraine understood. "Yes," Lorraine had said, "I wish there had been people like that to help me back in the day, y'know." And the two had hugged each other.

But Lorraine's generous offer had triggered another idea. Lew recalled that several residents whose birch trees had been stolen had offered a modest reward for any information leading the DNR to the thieves. She called the DNR officer and after he confirmed that Patterson and his motley crews were behind most of the illegal logging, Lew had said, "If Charlene Rotowski hadn't been forthcoming about the actions of her ex-husband, we might still be looking for the miscreants. I think she deserves that reward money." And the DNR officer had agreed.

"Chief," Bruce called from where he was threading fly line through the guides on his fly rod, "I'm about to have that lesson from Peter on long casting. You wanna watch in case he does it wrong?"

"Sure, but I'll bet Peter knows what he's doing," said Lew, sitting down to watch.

"Bruce, the good news is you're starting with the right gear," said Peter, "five-weight is the standard fly rod for New Zealand trout, too. Then, 'cause we cast long when we're sight fishing, I like to use a weight-forward taper and a longer leader so I can load the rod with a good twenty-five feet of line."

"What about tippet?" asked Lew, referring to the end section of fly line that would need to be added onto the leader.

"A 4X tippet is fine," said Peter. "If you're hoping to land a good-size trout like eleven pounds or more, you want a tippet strong enough to handle a fish that size."

Then the coaching began and Lew listened, relieved that she wasn't the instructor trying to straighten out Bruce's struggle with his double haul. Osborne, who had squeezed in to sit beside her, was focused on everything Peter was saying.

"Does what I'm telling Bruce make sense to you, Chief?" asked Peter as he watched Bruce execute a forward cast that plopped disconcertingly close to the pontoon.

"It does with one addition," said Lew. "When I instruct I emphasize body motion. Shift your weight backward on the backcast and follow through forward like you're throwing a ball. Peter, when it comes to casting a long line, I follow what my teacher, the famous Joan Wulff, taught me: *count* on body motion."

"What trout fly would you suggest right now, Lew?" asked Osborne. "I've got that nice buggy-looking Firefly that you tied for me last winter—"

"Gee, Doc, with Gray Drake's hatching along the shoreline and Loon Lake's dark water—I'd stick with an Adams, maybe a size eighteen."

"Oh yeah? I fish Adams all the time," said Peter, "great reliable dry fly, whatever hemisphere you fish in." And he laughed.

Jessie walked over in time to watch Bruce make a better forward cast, this time dropping his trout fly soundlessly. Water flashed and to Bruce's amazement he had a small bluegill on his line.

"Jessie," said Peter, "would you help me release that bluegill? I'll use forceps while you cradle the little guy. Be sure to keep its head and gills in the water so I can get that barbless hook out without hurting him."

"Not to worry. Dad showed me how," said Jessie, leaning over the side of the pontoon with the net. "We can do this."

Lew watched the two as they caught, cradled, and released the little fish. Then she checked on Osborne, who was busy tying an Adams onto his tippet. That left Molly alone up front with Ray.

———————

Lew motioned for Ray to let her take over steering the pontoon. He nodded, getting the message that she wanted time alone with the older sister. Settling into the captain's chair, Lew glanced over at Molly, who still had her feet up, lounging on the bench with a sun hat pulled down over her eyes.

"Will it take long to settle the estate questions now that both your father and stepmother are . . . gone?" asked Lew.

"A while, I'm sure," said Molly, straightening up and swinging around to place her bare feet on the floor of the pontoon. Brushing her hair out of her eyes, she leaned forward, elbows on her knees as she watched the shoreline go by.

"I'll be flying back up here off and on over the next few months. Have to sell the house and stuff."

"Sell everything?" asked Lew.

"No, Jessie and I will divide the antiques that were my mom's and we'll divide up my dad's fly rods and his fly-fishing gear. The rest we'll sell."

The two women were quiet for a while, the pontoon motor humming as the boat sailed along over the glassy surface of the lake.

"I was wondering, Chief Ferris, if you and Dr. Osborne might be up for letting me go fly-fishing with you? Maybe show me the streams you like? I never did have a chance to fish up here with my dad."

"I would like that," said Lew. "Say, Molly, if you don't mind, there's something I'd like to share with you, something that happened to me twelve years ago."

Molly said nothing. She kept her eyes on Lew.

"My son, Jamie, was stabbed to death in a bar fight when he was seventeen. Jamie was drunk, he'd pulled a knife and started the fight, which I'm sorry to say was a pattern of bad behavior he'd picked up from his father.

"The boy who stabbed him didn't mean to. He had grabbed the knife away from Jamie and was walking away when Jamie tripped him and as the boy fell he swung around and the knife nicked Jamie's jugular.

"So my son died in a bar parking lot. Now . . ." Lew looked down at her hands and paused before saying, "I could have been furious with the boy who stabbed him but I understood how it happened. I think about this often and wonder what I could have done to prevent that from happening. Certainly I should never have married a man like his father but that's easy to say today.

"Where I'm going with my story is this. If my son had died at the hands of someone who *wanted* him dead for his own selfish reasons . . . If there had been deliberate malicious intent—I would have gone after that person. It's a primal urge: *I would have made him pay.*"

"Umm," said Molly, her eyes never leaving Lew's. "So you know." Molly spoke with a hint of uncertainty.

"What I *know*"—Lew emphasized the word—"is that the aviation officials have ruled that egregious carelessness due to the plane's owner not following repair and inspection procedures is what led to the crash of Gordon Maxwell's plane.

"Now, if you want *my* point of view on the crash *and* what led up to it," said Lew, "Gordon Maxwell killed himself."

Molly pulled her feet back up on the bench, stretched out, and set her sun hat back over her eyes. The pontoon motored on. Two Jet Skis buzzed in the distance, a dragonfly hovered over Molly's hat, its wings capturing the sun and its huge eyes reflecting the blue sky, the clouds: life.

Lew, watching her, wondered if the young woman was satisfied. Lew hoped so. She felt she knew what was in Molly's heart: someone needs to know that Gordon Maxwell did not get away with the murder of my father.

Molly knew that Lew knew. That was enough.

At the back of the boat, Bruce kept struggling. Osborne's double haul worked for the first time. Peter sat down to watch the two men. Ray fished in his hamper for the egg salad sandwiches. And Jessie helped him set out the lunch.

ACKNOWLEDGMENTS

A warm thank-you to everyone who has worked to make me look good: my editor, Jackie Cantor; her assistant, Sara Quaranta; our copy editor; our production team; and, of course, my wonderful agent, Martha Millard.